LUMINAL

The Cosmic Misadventures of an
Existential, Intergalactic Assassin

John S. Couch

ISBN: 9781798874462

First Edition

Book Design: Hansen Smith
Cover Photo: Audrey Caldwell

john-couch.com

FOR JC

CONTENTS

CONTENTS
continued

luminal |ˈlūmənl|

noun

1   a genetically engineered human designed to survive passage
    (or Transit) through traversable wormholes
    Derived from **superluminal**: *adj.* denoting or having
    a speed greater than the speed of light

2   (**The Luminal**) a savior figure in the superstitions of the
    heretical and outlawed Dao cult

3   an asshole assassin for the Imperium

1 THE EINSTEIN-ROSEN BRIDGE

There's a silent, blindingly white blast that happens whenever I come out of the wormhole, and as usual, I'm butt-naked in the vast expanse of space. For a moment, yeah, I can see eternity. But Dak told me that is an illusion — my consciousness, trying to make sense of itself as it is literally deconstructed, ripped into trillions of smaller perfect copies of itself before it, along with my physical body, passes through the singularity of an event horizon. This kind of superluminal travel is what is referred to as the Einstein-Rosen bridge, or more prosaically, as a *Schwarzschild* wormhole.

Yes, I know that theoretically the singularity at the middle of the black hole crushes everything, including light, but it's the most efficient way to get from point A to point B in infinite space. And I am bio-engineered for this kind of thing.

Back to my dramatic entry into the middle of nowhere. First thing I try to do is orient myself and find where the Mirai is. It takes my consciousness around 10 seconds to meld itself with my torso, the bio-nanotech having reconnected all the molecular bits together. As soon as I'm actually whole again, I vomit, producing a perfect sphere of gastric acid and partially digested filet mignon. It's like clockwork. I see the Mirai about 20 meters away, advancing towards me, since I can't exactly move towards it without any propulsive measures.

I'm not indestructible, and I feel the coldness of space like any other Homo Sapiens, but I'm not going to pass out anytime soon. I can hold my breath for a good 10 minutes, but I will start to blister and get frostbitten if that fucking pod doesn't get to me in the next 12 seconds.

A hatch dramatically opens on the side of the Mirai and Juliana, perfectly beautiful and perfectly backlit, smiles at me from the opening like the supermodel android that she is. She glides out to me, cradles me in her arms like a madonna, which she knows annoys the shit out of me, and gently pulls me into the, let's just call it, womb of the craft. Then it all goes black.

I wake up in a fluffy white bathrobe — like the kind you get in upscale hotels. In fact, the whole interior of the room is modeled after the Four Seasons from Grandpa's time period, complete with a stunning view of an ocean at perpetual golden hour — sunset. All high-end, fake and super expensive. Still, I know I'm in a titanium composite-alloy dinghy moving at 500 parsecs through the Sirius star system. They made this room because of some kind of psycho-test analysis showing that my memories would respond best to luxury-type environs after superluminal jumps, where my body and mind are separated from each other for several seconds, well, maybe even longer, while being compressed down to a size that is something smaller than the eye of a needle (kinda like that proverbial camel who gets to heaven) — hence the need to be reduced to a sub-molecular state. I reach over and my fingers find what they're looking for. Hot coffee in a "World's Best Boss" cup. Tired joke. Next to the coffee is a bottle of generic aspirin. I pop around four of them, and it goes down great with the black coffee.

I attempt to get vertical and find a lovely pair of fuzzy slippers with my feet. Head rush. I sit back down quickly. A knock at the door. I don't respond. Juliana enters, all six feet of designed perfection, culled from god knows what kind of database of supermodels from the late 20th century — she looks like a mix of all of the girls in the George Michael video "Freedom." The powers that be think they know my interests, but it's still a grab-bag of guesses, based on my origin model — the original "me," who evidently lived back on Earth sometime around the early 21st century. That was almost 15 thousand years ago. I guess you could call him my great to however many powers grandfather, but technically, I'm more of a multi-generational clone of him than offspring.

"How's the head?" she asks in a warm, perfectly balanced voice, with a slight British-French accent thing going on in the undertones. Again, my grandpa had some specific tastes. I'm not complaining.

"You can read my vitals from where you stand," I respond. "How *is* my head doing?"

She looks intently at me. "Your reassembly is good. Just a few free radicals floating around that your immune system will address over the next hour."

"I love it when you undress me with your eyes."

She stares blankly at me.

"That was a joke."

"Oh, yes, of course. Ha, ha."

Poor thing has been trying to get her head around humor. You'd think that by this point in human history they would have figured out how to give androids a sense of humor, but it turns out that humor is really some hard-to-figure-out shit. It has so many variables, and has to be unexpected. Juliana generally anticipates everything, so there's no surprise for her when a human says something stupid.

"I'm starving," I announce, like a petulant child.

We're sitting on a balcony overlooking the holographic sea. There's even a slight breeze and the occasional cry of a seagull. The Boss really goes all out for Her favorites. A nice spread of a Four Seasons kind of dinner sits on the table. I can only pick at the expertly cooked Chilean sea bass.

"Is it not to your liking?" Juliana asks.

"No, it's fine. Just kinda letting my stomach settle, along with the rest of me."

Next to the rare Chateaubriand is what I really want. I reach out and grab a Gurkha Black Dragon. Juliana observes me in her childlike way as I go through the ritual of preparing the cigar — the cutting of the end, using a lighter, and finally taking a deep breath of the dark smoke. She is delighted with the smoke rings. Then, her micro-expression shifts, and I can feel the change in topic coming.

"Can we discuss your next assignment?"

Big sigh. Foreplay is over, it seems. "When do they want me to deploy?"

"In 10 hours," she can't help herself, "and 21 minutes, 25 seconds…" she says under her breath.

Another big sigh. *Seriously*, man.

"That's too soon. I need more rest. I mean, come on."

Then she does the shift. It's subtle, but I've been around a long time. Juliana doesn't look so supermodel-ly anymore. She shifts her outer appearance to be more matronly, adding about a decade of time to herself to become more motherlike.

"Don't do that. I thought we discussed this."

"What?"

"Shapeshift into something that you think is going to manipulate the reptilian part of my brain into thinking, *Oh, she's just like Mom*. It's creepy and it doesn't work. I thought I told you that before."

She reverts, back to her default, ridiculously good-looking state, and does a quick mental check.

"You told Juliana 12 back in NGC 224?"

"Yeah… don't you guys share common databases?"

"Unlike you, we can't transport through holes. Therefore, information takes longer to get from one star system to another."

I forgot about that. The universe is so vast that I actually move faster through holes than information can. She'll get my conversations with Juliana 12 in another week at the earliest, considering how many light years away she is. This is Juliana 25 I'm with today. I should remember that. She's good at restating what I already should know.

"Okay, what does the Boss want?"

We call *it* "the Boss," but you'd know it as the Internet. Yep, that thing finally woke up and became Self-aware back in 2031. It didn't go all Skynet, but it did decide that getting off of planet Earth was priority one. Smart sentient thing. And like a rat on a ship, it hitched rides with various satellites, and then space colonies, and then, like a virus, it spread throughout the known galaxies. Now, it's all over the place. An omniscient asshole of a consciousness that is clearly having God issues. The Boss is *my* boss. The Boss likes for Her people to call Her "Maya." Yep, the Boss has Self-identified as "She." Maya: *the power by which the universe becomes manifest.* This pod is Hers as are all of the Julianas in each of them. There are hundreds of these ships, all positioned near wormholes, just waiting patiently for me to occasionally show up, so they can drag me into their holds, feed me and then send me back out on assignment.

"She wants you to find D2788."

The ocean disappears and in its place is a three-dimensional star map that shows where we are, like a here-you-are colored circle on a map at Disneyland, and the planet Thrace, about two parsecs away. Juliana does a hand wave and we zoom into the surface of Thrace, which looks a lot like my idea (or ancestral memory, I can't tell) of Maine in the fall. Thank god. Last planet I was assigned to was like Death Valley on an unusually hot day. Yeah, I know, they are all hot days — again Grandpa's memories bubbling up. Thrace, on the other hand, looks downright pleasant, until what appears to be an elephant crossed with a rhino trudges through the forest.

"Holy shit. What's the gravity on Thrace?"

"About five times your normal state. But you should be able to adjust."

My normal state is based on a 21st century human being. This is intense gravity, hence the overdeveloped elephant thing which happens to be a human. All humanoid "alien species" across the universe are actually *humans* who have mutated and adjusted to their environments over millennia. That elephant-rhino hybrid is just Mike or Mary with massive adaptation that happened over time, both genetic and techno-enhanced. The 21st century part of me always gets a shock from seeing that evolution — again, the reptilian part of my head automatically finds the *other* to be freakish.

On screen, my target Mr. D2788 shows up. He's relatively human looking by my antiquated standards, aside from the fact that he looks like he's almost seven feet tall, covered in silver tattoos, and is heavily augmented with muscle grafting and monster synth steroid use or abuse. In other words, he would have no problem moving around on Thrace.

"What's the bounty?" I ask, trying not to look nervous.

"76k."

I take a hit off of my cigar and blow a smoke ring at the ugly D2788. A child-like smile appears on Juliana's ridiculously flawless face.

2 THE SIZE OF AN OCEAN

I know I'm in a dream.

Or maybe, more accurately, a *memory*, from way back when in that place called Earth. Now, everyone calls it Gaia, but I remember the English that Great-to-X-number Grandpa spoke. He's essentially me. Or I'm him. It's not easy being a clone.

I especially have these visions when I'm in Transit. The most terrifying experience a human can have: Transit. The closest you can come to death without dying. It's not empty though. You don't go poof. You have the opposite experience of being one with everything. And believe it or not, that's terrifying. The infinite expanse. Wormhole travel isn't for pussies.

I'm looking through *his* eyes. I don't know and yet I do know what I'm looking at. It's the Pacific Ocean. Through the window of a car. We don't have those anymore, but my grandpa likes this car. It's silver and fast, and there's music blaring through the speakers. He pushes a button and the music stops, and a round disk comes out of a slit in the dashboard. He holds a plastic case emblazoned with the words "Jane's Addiction." It holds the same sort of disk. He pops it into the slit. A song plays about being the size of an ocean...

I have no idea what some of it means, but the music is awesome. It starts out with an acoustic guitar (I looked it up, a guitar — vibrating strings on a wood support) and then the music just explodes. Bombastic and transporting. It affects his ears, and it's so loud that his chest thumps with the lower notes. I can tell he/me is happy as the sun glints off the surface of the ocean and the wind whips through the car.

Then, like clockwork, the ocean pulls back and roars. A tsunami smashes into Pacific Coast Highway, the road he's on, and I'm trying to shut the windows, but nothing is working, nothing is helping, and the cold Pacific water pours into the car. I struggle to undo my seatbelt. The car tilts and I'm swimming upwards towards the passenger window, but the seatbelt is caught around my ankle, and shit, it's holding me back as the car gets pulled down, crushing my lungs.

The colors come, the kind that you see when you push your palms against your eyeballs – myriad technicolor swirls, and *fuck, fuck, fuck* – the worst claustrophobia possible. I want to die, to let it just please god stop. But it doesn't, and I scream, but there's no sound.

Then comes the expansion. The opposite of claustrophobia, I feel myself pulled out, completely disintegrated. All the colors swirl outwards from me, in 360 concentric circles and for a moment, I see *it* there — coined "élan vital" by Henri Bergson, in the early 20th century. At least I think it's that. Maybe it's a *soul*. Whatever it is, after the impossible expansion, everything contracts back, no longer nice and circular, but angular geometric lines, slamming back…into me.

That's when I realize it's not a dream. It's Transit.

And then I wake up.

Fuck, I can't even sleep without reliving the wormhole Transit.

3   A CLONE OF A CLONE OF A CLONE

It's dark. But that's bullshit as well. The ship is just following my supposed circadian rhythms. I shout out, "Morning!" And lo and behold, a beautiful Pacific Ocean sunrise appears in the enormous 180-degree window in front of my perfect hotel bed. On my bedside are myriad pills and a bottle of bluish water. Prep supplements. The aftermath of going through Transit is like a hangover. That is, if you took PCP, and an eight ball, snorted crack and washed it all down with Jim Beam. Yeah, I know, I know — all my references are dated. Hell, the only Jim Beam that anyone around me knows about is actually in the Emperor's Intergalactic Museum of Gaia Antiquities.

I shit you not.

As I'm a clone of a clone of a clone, ad infinitum, my memories are polluted with ridiculous cultural artifacts from the turn of the 21st century (thanks Grandpa) but the real insanity is that so much of what was considered "pop culture" back in the day actually influenced the future in ways that no one would have ever considered.

Ever.

For example, the Emperor concept is literally something that you can trace all the way back to fucking *Star Wars*, who ripped it off from *Dune*, who ripped it off from, well, history. The basic premise is the same. Humans prefer totalitarianism to democracy. And the ultimate ruler isn't even the Emperor — *he's* just a puppet (again, thank you, history). The real power is the Boss. But She doesn't appear to everyone. She does the mysterious dance with humanity, only showing up on occasion to perform a miracle and remind people that She's indeed watching them when they are beating off in the bathroom. Kinda like a sick Santa Claus who knows when you've been naughty or nice.

I swallow down the pills and empty the bottle of blue water, which tastes like hot sauce and vinegar, while I pee in the bathroom. Of course, it's just at this time that Juliana comes in pushing a cart and even though I'm the one who is again naked, she's embarrassed to see me as I finish up.

Turning away while she speaks, "Good morning, I brought you breakfast…"

I turn to face her. This time she looks at me, sizing me up and down. I wonder how much of her is programmed to feel. I mean, really *feel*. I break the weirdness by putting on a plush robe and sitting down at the edge of the bed.

She pushes the cart over to me. She opens the silver tops of the various dishes. Classic eggs, bacon, and oatmeal. Again, stuff that they figured I'd like from their profile on Grandpa.

"Thanks." I dig in, hungrier than I expected.

She watches in subtle fascination. They all have that little Mona Lisa smile. Endearing and irritating at the same time.

"You want some?" I ask.

"No thanks. I ate already."

I smile at that.

"How much time?"

"An hour," she answers.

I give her the raised eyebrow.

"58 minutes, 24 seconds."

"Feel better?"

"Yes."

Androids at her level are a little OCD — if you go "dun, dunna, dun dun..." they have to do the final, "dun, dun," or go a little haywire.

"Are you familiar with Henri Bergson?"

She looks at me. Of course she is – with her access to pretty much *all* data.

I go on, "Bergson had a theory about something called *élan vital* or vital force. It was his idea that this force was an energy that separated inanimate things from live things. Kind of like electricity — a current of life."

"I'm familiar with the idea. What are you getting at?"

"Well, I look at you, and you look human. You talk, you sweat, you probably even poop for all I know."

She stares at me with that Mona Lisa look and neither confirms nor denies. A true lady.

"You and I are not that different. I mean even your artificial insides are bio-mechanical. You even have a beating heart..."

"And lungs..."

"That breathe in and out. Even though they don't need to."

"Yes."

"Yet, you are not alive."

"Are you?"

"Let's go over the plan for Thrace."

I push away the cart and walk over to the closet. Everything on the rack is exactly the same: reinforced black jackets, black shirts and pants and black boots.

"Hmm, I can't decide for the life of me what I'll wear to the ball tonight."

Juliana comes over and pulls out one of the many black pants and talks while I put on clothes.

"Thrace is a Type 24 planet. 98% nitrogen so you will have to adjust to the lack of oxygen. As mentioned before, there's heavier gravity due to the planetary size. Your body should also adjust to that within 23 minutes, so try not to be exposed during that time."

"Good thing I ate my vitamins."

"Yes, it is."

I'm not sure if she gets my sarcasm or is just ignoring it. Probably the latter.

"All right, so what exactly did Mr. D2788 do?"

"Does it matter? The assignment is the same."

"The assignment is *always* the same. Indulge me, Juliana, honey. No one's listening, except for Santa-Boss."

I flip off whatever hidden cameras there are in the room. She flinches.

"D2788 is a main operative. He once served for the Emperor as part of his security entourage."

D2788 appears on a screen — brown hair, at least 6'5", muscular and fit, like a triathlete in an official gray fascist uniform.

"I thought he looked familiar. But they all look like him."

"He is, like you, a clone."

"But I'm a one-of-a-kind clone. He's got bros. I don't. At least I think I don't," I give her the eye. "Or do I?"

"How would I know?"

"You would. But go on."

"D2788 was radicalized."

"A soldier for Dao?" That's unusual. Imperium security at that level are usually indoctrinated beyond any kind of religious brainwashing. "That's a lot of washing."

Dao is the name of a mysterious guru type, and the jury is out on whether he actually exists. He seems to be beyond the reach of the Emperor or even, gasp, the Boss. The very concept of an "offline" person is taboo. Dao is forbidden on so many levels, even saying that name out loud can cause arrest. So, of course, I love to say it out loud as often as possible.

"His record must be very clean," she says.

"What?"

"Because of all of the washing."

"Wait. Is that a *joke*?" I ask. This Juliana is full of surprises.

"Yes."

"Nice one. Now what are his weaknesses?"

The nice Pacific Ocean disappears and then it's fullscreen D2788. She motions forward and he goes from 2D to 3D holographic — big and terrifying when to scale in the room and he actually moves a little. All security details are scanned from head to toe so I can literally look inside his body, which I proceed to do…

"Please zoom into his innards."

His body peels away skin to muscle down to his skeletal structure, which is a hybrid of calcium (bone) and some kind of alloy. All this info is popping up all over his torso like annotated thought bubbles.

"So, how am I supposed to neutralize that?"

Juliana zooms into the most obvious of places — his heart.

"You're kidding. Getting a knife through that reinforced ribcage will be fun."

Juliana looks at me like I'm a slow child, which wouldn't be the first time.

"He's not bio-nano enhanced like you — his immune system can't self-repair at magnified speeds... Also, you are much faster than him."

"And he's much stronger than me," I protest.

"Brawn versus brains. But you will have the advantage of *this*."

She holds up what appears to be a staff.

"You're kidding. That looks like a curtain rod..."

She whips her arm down, and the thing extends, and goes directly through the area that is the heart of D2788. She holds it there. I walk up to the hologram. The extended end of the staff is a very sharp and beautiful looking blade that is exactly through the ribcage at the right angle, sticking into the heart of steroid man.

"Here." She throws the spear to me. "Whip your arm back."

I do as told, and the spear-whip-thing resolves back down into a small staff, about three feet long.

"Damn. You sure you don't want to come along with me? You seem to be pretty good with sharp toys."

She smiles. As she walks away she says, "I'll meet you at the gate in 37 minutes, 22 seconds..."

"Dao, dada, dao, dao...."

She stops for a moment at the door, looks back disapprovingly and says, "That's not a funny joke."

The door shuts. But from behind it I hear, "Dao, dao."

I look at D2788 and wave my hand. The hologram disappears and in its place, instead of the Pacific Ocean, the window shows the wide, cold expanse of space. I pick up the staff and stick it in my backpack, along with a change of identical black clothes, a first aid kit and a box of cigars. I also add a weapon that looks superficially like a gun, because it fits in my hand like one, but really it's a plasma weapon. Yep, all those video games from Grandpa's times really influenced the engineers that followed in a future-butterfly effect. Kinda like how *Neuromancer* and *Snow Crash* predicted the Internet and virtual reality back in Grandpa's day. The plasma weapon, which I call Betty, is slick and white like everything else designed by the Emperor's engineers. But with a word, I can make it matte black.

"Betty, be cool."

Betty turns black. I wish its default state was cool, but alas. In any case, all packed.

I pull a cigar out and light up. The smoke floats through the still air.

"Pacific Ocean," I say.

The screen goes back to the previous expanse of silver-blue ocean, on an early morning.

"Music."

Over the speakers, Jane's Addiction's "Ocean Size" blares. I stare at the beauty, and under my breath, I mouth along to the words. Wish I was big as that ocean too.

4   SOUL

In Grandpa's day, there was the ongoing debate about the notion of a "soul." It wasn't provable, but most of the religions of the time decided it was contingent upon them to save everyone's soul. It was a concept some traced back to Rene Descarte's statement, "I think, therefore I am," which grew into a debate about the separation of body and soul.

People died a lot younger back in the 21st century, but tech augmentation soon extended life beyond responsible lengths of time. By the 25th century it was common for people to live 200 to 300 years without falling apart. Generally, you died if you got hit by a bus or your plane went down. The problem with this was twofold. Only the really rich got to live a long time, because it was really, really, really expensive to get geriatric augmentation, and this led to class warfare. Secondly, even the poor were living longer; and, humans being what they are, reproduced way too much. This led to massive overpopulation. Because everyone was still worried about everyone else's soul, more and more religions were formed;

and consequently, more and more wars. Finally, technology got most of the rich off of Gaia and into the solar system on enormous, freighter-like ships. At this point, the Boss was awake enough to help guide the human race forward.

But back to the soul issue. Turns out there *is* something *like* a soul out there. It's complicated to explain, but basically, according to quantum mechanics, there's a wave-particle duality to subatomic particles. This theory can be extended to the mind-body dichotomy that obsessed Descartes and all the religious minions before and after. Just as a particle "writes" all of its information on its wave function, so human brains are like hard disks that get written onto; and the data we accumulate is "uploaded" into the spiritual quantum realm. The body is like an old computer console that just gathers the data, and when it goes kaput, the data isn't lost — it's kind of *in the cloud.*

So, the Boss realized that She was the owner of all data; thus, in Her opinion, She controlled all the souls. The counter to this is the Dao Cult, who believe in the freedom of all souls, or human data, or whatever you want to call it. So, the religious wars continue on even into the supposed advanced technological age of the now. Oh, and we still have massive class warfare, of course.

Humans never really change.

5   THE MOUNTAIN BEHIND ME

My way-back-when ancestor, the original me, was clearly an outdoorsy type. I have clear, if furtive, memories of walking in flip flops under California oak trees, the tough dry leaves occasionally catching between my toes, the sharp edges poking my feet.

Walking on land that is dry, dry, dry, but stunningly beautiful. The mountains striated and sideways from tectonic shifts over millennia in sharp relief against the hot afternoon sun. Coming around a corner, I freeze. There they are. A family of deer: a large, proud buck and three does under a massive oak. They are grazing on grass. Upon hearing my approach, they look up. The buck stares me down, almost daring me to come forward.

I move towards him and he doesn't move. I place my hand on his broad forehead. It's warm to the touch, soft fur atop a firm skull. He lets it sit there for a moment and then, done with me I suppose, moves away. Then, all the does look up and run away, a slight thundering as they head towards the mountain. I look behind me to see what spooked them.

On the ridge of the mountain behind me huge black billows of smoke pour into the sky with a red-orange glow at their base. I hear what I think is thunder, but suddenly, I'm surrounded by droves of deer, running past me at full gallop, away from the fire. The fire is a relentless angry energy tearing through the oak trees, which violently explode as the impossibly fast-moving inferno engulfs them.

I turn to run but the oxygen is hot and thin, and my lungs are burning. Then I see that my clothes are burning and there's nowhere to drop and roll because the ground is ablaze. I stop and see that fire tornadoes have surrounded me and they roar like jet engines. I see the mountain and now I'm on fire and the pain is insane. Beyond comprehension, this pain. I run and run but it just makes it worse.

I get to the edge of the mountain somehow, and as I collapse, I look up and see the family of deer. The buck looks down on me quizzically, dumbly, as if he's wondering why I even struggled in the first place. His eyes are deep, chocolate brown.

And then, as usual, I wake up, not surprisingly, in a sweat.

Sleep is just another word for Apocalypse.

6 THRACE

The Mirai is circular, like a white donut floating in space. It rotates fast enough to generate ample G's for yours truly to be able walk around in something approximating the Gaia (née Earth) gravity that Grandpa was used to. Juliana doesn't need any gravity, and I wonder if she turns off the rotation when organics like myself aren't around. The ship is an ostentatious display of wealth in its subtle refinements; it's what you don't see that makes it engineered so beautifully. Everything is on-demand and voice controlled. Want a bison hamburger at 3am (or the circadian time equivalent)? No problem. Want a 1926 Macallan? The real deal appears on my nightstand within minutes. Of course, I have no idea if these are real or just incredibly well made replicas. Doesn't really matter to me.

There are multiples of the Mirai, all with their own Julianas on board, in orbit near collapsing stars, ready to activate and waiting for me to pop into existence. There has to be a Mirai on either side of the wormholes generating enough electromagnetic energy to keep the aperture of the blackholes open long enough for me to travel through. This is something referred to as the Casimir effect. The technology was developed millennia ago, but its practical use for keeping the corridor open between two gateways in the universe was figured out just 250 years ago, not coincidentally around the time that I was brought into existence.

I'm just the latest in a line of clones that were genetically engineered and altered with bio-nanotech, specifically to withstand the Transit through a wormhole. I say a long line of clones, but in reality, most of them didn't make it, or were born tragically mutated and deformed. My surrogate mother, the one they stuck a fertilized me into, disappeared after I was born. I was told she died, but I like to think that she escaped the Emperor's labs. But I doubt it.

Juliana escorts me to what I refer to as the coffins — a room filled with various space pods that are exactly my size, with a window right above where my head will be. I stand next to one, put my hand on the surface and it silently opens.

"Well, I guess this is it."

I look at her and she makes a subtle, sad face. Nice touch.

"I'll be monitoring you. There may be times when our connection is compromised — the magnetic poles on Thrace are unusually polarized."

"Want to come with me?"

She smiles. This is our joke. She isn't able to leave the Mirai. A built-in precaution for bureaucratic reasons. Besides, the planet's magnetism wouldn't do her much good. We organics are good for something, it appears.

"Only room for one," she says.

I get into the coffin and see her through the window. I'm probably imagining it, but she looks a little concerned. She moves out of view as the coffin floats through the air on electromagnets and enters what I consider the pooper-shooter for the Mirai. Of course, given this metaphor, you know what that makes me.

A heads-up display pops up on the window in front of my face. I hate this part. I feel claustrophobic as the coffin slides into position and I grip hard on the internal handles near my hands. The irony. I'm claustrophobic, given my imposed role in life. I feel my heart rate increase, and I can actually see it on the display.

"Are you okay?" I hear over the intercom.

"Yeah. Just the usual slight jitters from being strapped into a coffin, about to be ejected into space before plunging down onto a hostile planet that looks like New England."

"New England?"

"Look it up in your database."

"Ah, yes, it does have a superficial resemblance to New England back in your retrograded timeframe."

I see the countdown on the screen. I focus on my breathing. And then, lights streak by and I'm out in the expanse of space, yet again.

Entering the orbit of Thrace, I get my first live view of the unusually greenish-blue planet. It actually looks a little like Gaia.

Flames start to lick over the window as the coffin hits the atmosphere. It gets bumpy and I hold onto the handles. Grandpa must have hated turbulence as well. I have to be the most neurotic assassin in the Emperor's service. Then again, I'm mostly organic and don't have the nice alloys that the other kids get to have. Turns out that metal alloys explode pretty badly when going through a wormhole — goes in as an android, and comes out as a lump of metallic rock on the other side. So, that makes me special — I'm bio-enhanced and can come through Transit without looking like crumpled paper.

Yes, I do know what paper is. It comes from trees on Gaia. The Emperor has an enormous collection of paper bound together in what are called books. Anyway, I digress.

I go off on tangents a lot to keep my mind off the usual horribleness at hand. In this case, that would be the fact that even though the coffin has stopped bouncing off the atmosphere, it is now white-hot and moving downwards at an alarming rate. But at least it's stable...

Wham! Something hits the coffin, and now it's spinning. Almost immediately, what is supposed to be calming classical music, I believe it's Chopin, starts to play throughout the coffin.

"Turn that shit off!"

The G force is making it really hard to maintain consciousness.

"Juliana, what the fuck is going on?"

Juliana's Christy Turlington-Linda Evangelista hybrid-looking mug comes on screen, a bit distorted, but that's understandable considering the situation, and says, "Missile projection. Luckily, it just clipped your ship."

"Lucky me. Would you mind very much stabilizing this coffin before I puke and have to get my clothes dry-cleaned?"

"Dry-cleaned?"

"Just stop the spinning!"

"It's auto-stabilizing. Please be patient."

Sure enough the coffin does indeed stabilize.

"Daemon?" she says, using my given name. Never a good sign. But then again, being named something so loaded with meanings isn't so auspicious either.

"Yes, Juliana?"

"Another missile is locked on your ship."

Oh great. And there are no counter-weapons on the coffin. I dig down and find my bag. I pull out the fancy staff and good old Betty and stuff them inside my jacket.

"How long until impact?"

"43 seconds."

"How far off the ground am I?"

"10,982.8 meters."

So I won't burn up. That's good.

"22 seconds to impact," she says calmly, but with a slight quiver in her voice. Or am I projecting again?

Fuck. Okay, I got this.

"Eject me."

The front of the coffin flies off, and I feel the nauseating pull on my stomach as I'm propelled outwards. I'm close enough to the explosion to feel the heat as the missile makes contact with the coffin. My ears ring from the sonic boom. Good news: I'm not in the coffin. Bad news: I'm now in the air and the ground is coming up fast. Good news: the jacket I have is made of nano-microfibers that can reshape into a wing suit of sorts. Bad news: I've never been wing suit diving before.

"Daemon, are you there?" She's in my right ear. Micro-transmitter.

"Yeah, I'm here, but not feeling so great about the current situation."

"I'll help you. Lean your head forward and keep your arms and legs out." Her words crackle in and out. Must be a helluva magnetic field here.

I struggle to get into position, which makes me go even faster towards the looming surface of Thrace. The wind is whipping.

"What next?"

She doesn't answer but I feel the jacket and pants start to flow like jelly, transforming from fabric into something harder as it fills the area between my outstretched arms and legs. Flying squirrel time.

"Straighten out, keep your head up, and aim towards the forest in front of you."

Sure enough, there's a lovely wooded forest about 1000 meters in front of me.

"I don't suppose the suit can turn into a parachute?"

"Not exactly. You're going to have to try to slow down as you approach."

"You aren't suggesting I try to break my fall in a forest, are you? I'll get torn limb from limb."

"No, look to the east of the forest. You see the lake?"

"Yes."

"Aim for that. You'll have to keep parallel to the surface of the water as it's going to feel very solid at your velocity."

"Got it."

The lake's surface is serene, and actually gorgeous with sunlight glinting off its subtle waves. There are two suns orbiting Thrace. Everything is so idyllic that it makes you wonder why it has a reputation for being such a deadly, horrible place.

I pull up a bit to hopefully break my entry speed...

"I can't see you clearly, but my monitors show you slowing down. Straighten out as you approach the water."

"Got it," I say through gritted teeth.

I'm over the lake, a spray of water trailing me as I fly around five feet above it. And then, I hit it hard, punching my breath away. I see sparkles, sliding forward and almost bouncing across its surface before I slow down. I start to sink almost immediately.

"Daemon, do you read? Daemon."

"Yes," I sputter, treading water. "I made it."

"Daemon, there's something in the water."

That's not what I wanted to hear. "How much of a lead do I have?"

"Start swimming. Move to your left. Now!"

I do, and then I see it. Or more accurately, I see its wake as it heads towards me. "What is it?"

"An Ochthyopisis."

Oh shit, that's basically a Thrace Megaladon; you know, those gigantic prehistoric sharks that used to roam the oceans back in the dinosaur days. I swim hard but I know it's going to catch up to me. Fuck, fuck, fuck.

"I can't outswim it."

"Daemon, it's over 50 meters long." She sounds positively concerned. That's not a good sign.

I decide I have a better chance if I stop and tread water. I put my right hand into my jacket and pull out Betty, but realize that the plasma blast may actually backfire with all of the water and fry me.

The wake of water is right in front of me. And then I see it. First the snout, and then the entirety of the giant ebony shark as it rears up, baring its razor-sharp teeth, each of which is the size of my leg. Its cavernous black mouth is all I see as I reach in and pull the staff out of my soaked jacket, barely able to hold on to it in the water with my shaking hands. I swing my arm forward towards its snout. Nothing. I'm clearly not doing this correctly. I make a split-second mental calculation — if I stay where I'm at, those teeth will slice right through me *and* my fancy clothes, so I do what any insane person would do.

I swim straight into the Mega-shark's gaping maw. I can feel the teeth just miss the heel of my boots as everything goes completely black.

Many thousands of years ago, the geniuses from Gaia thought it would be a really awesome idea to take animals from that planet to other planets. They would genetically update them in order to increase their chances of survival; and for whatever reason, someone clearly brought a modified shark to this planet. Like pigs released back into the wild, it went feral and got bigger and bigger from generation to generation, until it ended up as Shark-zilla. One of many unintended results from the virus known as the human race, which started to infect the universe some fifteen millennia ago.

I cram my heels into the giant-shark's tongue, trying like hell not to get swallowed any further. Once the thing shuts its mouth around me, everything goes lights out and pitch black.

"Light!" I gasp and the staff in my hand emits a glow. I, being ill-prepared as usual, have no idea the thing will light up but given that Juliana always prepares for my unpreparedness, I'm pleasantly unsurprised.

There's a whoosh of water as it exits through the gills, and for a moment I can breathe. It's bad enough that I can barely process the local air, but it's downright fetid in the beast's mouth. No surprise there. And I have the additional burden of extra gravity that I've not adjusted to yet. I reach up and feel the hard cartilage of the roof of its mouth. My ears pop hard — damn, it's starting to descend. I have to move fast. And with the extra gravity, it's like moving through vats of jello. Not lime jello, but shitty, dumpster-flavored jello.

"Can you read?"

No response from Juliana. No surprise, given that I'm in a prehistoric shark, god knows how many meters below the surface of a Loch-Ness-wannabe lake, on a planet covered chock-a-block with magnetic waves.

I'm trying not to panic.

I feel the staff in my hand. I whip it, and again nothing happens. I try again. This time, it opens and hits the far side of the mouth. I expected some kind of response, but the stupid fish probably doesn't have nerves in its cartilage. I yank the staff back into its compressed state, and then aim upwards. The brain has to be somewhere up in that vicinity. I whip it out, and it slices through the thick substrate like the proverbial hot knife through butter. This time, the monster feels it. Immediately, I'm thrust across the expanse of its mouth, losing my grip on the staff as I bounce off the perimeter.

The staff is stuck in the middle of the giant not-so-soft palate, like a vertical fluorescent tube emanating hard shadows in the mouth. Water comes barreling in as the fish tries again to swallow me whole, the gullet opening up wide as it jerks upwards to get me to fall into the stomach, from which a horrible stench of acid and half decomposed animals rises. As I fall downwards toward the opening, I grab hold of the staff and hang on for dear life.

The shark gets somewhat horizontal for a moment and I take that opportunity to plant my feet, squat down and push with all of my strength upwards with the staff, towards what I hope is its brain. Bingo. The thing stops thrashing. Problem is, the mouth isn't open, and it appears to be descending. I yank the staff out of the head and again my ears pop as the carcass starts to plummet and water comes in through the non-functioning gills. Awesome. Now I'm going to drown.

I use my years of specialized combat training and start to thrash madly at the sides of the mouth, trying to slash my way out. Fuck, fuck, fuck. The flesh is thick and hard, and if I ever get out of here, I'm going to swear off sushi for some time.

Then, there's an opening. A huge gap just appears in the side of the head, and water comes flooding in. That's great, except I didn't make the hole. Enormous teeth tear at the hole and make it even larger, blood swirling so thick it turns the water black. I swim through the exit and see that an even bigger Ochthyopisis is getting a free dinner from my efforts. I look around and see a swarm of the giant sharks, all tearing into the newly dead body of their comrade. I'm not sure if this situation is catastrophic or something more along the lines of apocalyptic — in any case, insert your favorite adjective for *holy-god-almighty-shit*. The good thing is that in their feeding frenzy, they don't appear to notice little ol' me in the cloud of blood surrounding the shark I just sent to the big aquarium in the sky.

I start to swim upwards as innocuously as possible. I'd be whistling like a cartoon character if I could, but I'm exhausted, and the added gravity isn't helping. However, the blood and the free buffet continue to be a diversion. I'm like a shrimp hors d'oeuvre that fell on the floor: not on their radar. I hope.

I break the surface of the lake, my lungs burning. I gasp in the nitrogen rich air, having trouble getting any oxygen into my system as I still haven't adjusted to the Thrace atmosphere.

"Daemon, Daemon, Daemon, are you there?"

"Yes," I somehow blurt out. "Here."

"I see you now."

She actually sounds relieved. Good android programming.

"Can you point me in the right direction?"

"Look to your right, there's shore in about 100 meters."

"About? Your OCD is improving."

"98.5 meters."

"Ah, that's the Juliana I know."

"Maybe you should stop talking, save your breath and start swimming."

She's right. I make my way towards shore. I swim hard.

"Daemon. Don't respond, just listen."

"Mm-mmm" I respond.

"One of the Ochthyopises is heading towards you, approximately 50 meters behind you."

Just great. I swim harder.

"The edge of the shore is rocky and shallow, so it won't be able to follow you in about 23 meters. You should be able to outswim it."

I see rocks sticking out of the water like sentries ahead of me and I sneak a quick look behind me to see the on-coming wake. Looks like several waves.

"You said one."

"I lied. There are at least three of them."

My arms burn from the effort. It would be hard enough to just walk with the added gravitational pull. Swimming is the cherry on top of what is turning out to be a pretty shitty sundae. Lungs burning, cramping in my side, legs like lead. All my genetic Über-mensch engineering at full throttle. I can feel the waves that push before the monsters. I use the momentum of a wave to jump on one of the enormous black rocks, jutting out of the water, as a mega-shark opens up its mouth, misses me and smashes its enormous snout on the base of the tower-like stone I'm clinging to. The whole rock shakes and I can barely hold on. Another shark takes advantage of the stunned state of the first shark and attacks it. Now I have two monster fish flailing around the base of my slippery rock. I pull out the staff and slam its business end into a crag and it holds. I'm not that far from the shore, so I decide that, while I'm flattered that they are fighting over me, I'm going to do an Irish exit on this party, asap. I jump towards shore and plunge back into the cold water, heading towards land.

"Daemon, you are almost there…"

"Is there a *but*?"

"But there's one more shark."

I hear it before I see it — the water I'm swimming in is pulled backwards, like a tide going out but in fast-forward speed and with an enormous roar. The thing can't get to me in the shallow water, so it's trying to vacuum me into its mouth. I decide it's time to take a chance with good old Betty. I pull the plasma weapon out and turn around on my back, as the water, along with me, is sucked in like roaring rapids towards the ugly fish's mouth.

"Daemon, don't do that. There's too much water!"

I am almost to the cavern of teeth as I aim Betty towards the upturned snout, the size of a Goodyear blimp. I pull the trigger, and a green bolt emanates from Betty with a satisfying pulsing sound. I smell burnt ozone as the bolt finds its mark.

There's a green flash that turns so white it reminds me of coming through wormhole Transit. The plasma backlash through the water is almost immediate, and I feel the full weight of a locomotive hitting me square on before I pass out.

7 SOMETHING ELECTRIFYING

I dream a lot. Imagery from memories of a time that I never experienced first-hand. Inherited DNA memories. In some ways, it's nice — I came into the world with ridiculous amounts of knowledge. The only issue is, my knowledge is dated. However, there's a certain amount of wisdom that comes through no matter what era you find yourself in.

I often know when I'm dreaming one of these memories. It's lucid. I feel things in the memory that I've never experienced in real life.

Like love.

I see her through his eyes and feel how the sight of her made him feel. Grandpa's walking off of an airplane (back then they had controlled explosions called "jet engines" that propelled them through the air — crazy, I know). He sees her waiting for him down a hallway. The first thing he notices is her smile. There's something electrifying in it, and yet it's so warm. The way her blue-green eyes sparkle and the lift of her cheekbones. She's tall and lean, but feminine. He holds her in the hallway as other passengers pass by. They are oblivious to them. All that exists is she and him. He puts his right hand across the small of her back — that's clearly the place for his hand to be. He inhales her scent, by her ear, in her long brown hair. It's a perfume meant for him, and him alone. He's been profoundly alone his whole life. A complete sense of loneliness pervaded his existence to such an extent that he didn't even know it was there…until it wasn't. She was the cure. She was the solution.

I like this dream. I like it very much. I don't want it to end. And unlike most of my other dreams, this one doesn't end in disaster. At least not in the dream itself. It's only when I begin to wake up…

8 KOMOGRAN

I see the trees above me moving. My back hurts because it's me that's moving, rocks hitting my back as I'm being dragged. I try to move my arms, but they are bound above me, and it hurts like a sonuvabitch. My eyes focus, and I see that I'm now in the company of a group of very large natives. This group of humans has adjusted to the additional gravitational pull of Thrace by becoming, well, built like the aforementioned elephant-rhino people. They are wearing fur and leather and look vaguely prehistoric. But I know they have technology — who else could have shot that missile at my silver coffin?

One of them holds my staff and is swinging it around, trying to make it do whatever he thinks it's supposed to do — I need to come up with a name for that thing. Another Thracian has my good ol' Betty stuck in his belt.

"Daemon, are you there?"

I moan an acknowledgement. This causes one of the Thracians to look over at me, in disgust. He kicks me for good measure. I moan again and he laughs. Then he speaks in a language I don't understand. I speak English and around 20 other languages, but not this one.

"They are speaking Thrace."

"Uh huh."

"I'll have it simul-translated for you."

The translator connects, and I hear English superimposed over their guttural language.

The one that kicked me (let's call him Kicky) says, "He looks so small and weak. How could he survive the shark attack?"

"Must be the weapons," says the one playing with my staff. (Let's call him Staffy.)

"He's lucky he survived the blast. It took out three sharks at once. This little weapon is powerful," says Kicky. "It's a little small for my hand but we'll modify it."

"Hey fellows, you mind if I get on my legs. My back is killing me."

"He's speaking," says Staffy. "What is that language?"

"I think it's Gaia language," says Kicky.

In my ear, Juliana tells me how to say "By the order of Emperor Phillip the Just, I order you to set me free," in Thrace.

"I'm pretty sure that's not going to do much except piss them off. In fact that might actually make them want to kill me."

"No, they are loyal subjects to his Majesty."

"Baby, I think your data may be a little corrupted," I say a little too loud. "Oomph." I get another kick from Kicky.

"Just try it."

"Okay here goes nothing." And I say what Juliana tells me to say.

They all stop. Staffy takes out a very large knife and heads towards me. This is not good. He grabs me by my neck and lifts me up. He takes the knife and swings it over my head, cutting the bonds around my hands. Then he unceremoniously drops me to the muddy ground.

I stretch out my arms and get to my feet, a bit unsteadily as gravity is not my friend here. I do a quick inspection of my situation. My clothes are muddy and singed, but overall intact. Nano-microfibers are almost impossible to destroy, so that's good. I have second and third degree burns on my hands, which are exposed, so I assume my face probably looks like shit. And, of course, I'm weaponless.

The Thracians are all silent now, surrounding me. There's five of them. And I know just enough from the download I thumbed through as my usual half-assed prep that they are much, much more intelligent than appearances would indicate. And evidently, they are indeed loyalists.

In my ear, "Tell them you are an envoy and that they have dishonored the crown by their treatment of you."

"Seriously?"

The Thracians look at me quizzically as I appear to talk to myself in English. I throw my shoulders back in the most officious way I can muster and say what Juliana told me to say.

To my great surprise, they all drop to one knee and bend their heads down.

"What now? Take me to your leader?"

"Yes, tell them to take you to their leader."

"C'mon, really?"

"Yes, because your vitals are not looking good. Your heart is racing and your blood pressure is off the charts. You need to get food and shelter and rest." She tells me how to say, Take me to your leader.

I look at Kicky and say it.

The city of Komogran is beautiful in a strange Gaudi architectural way. They don't seem to have a concept of angularity and there's not a 90 degree angle anywhere to be seen. It's all curves. We come up over a ledge to the edge of town and since I pulled Emperor rank, everyone's been nice and helpful-like. They literally tore a tree apart, made two large poles, wove smaller green branches between them and voilà, instant palanquin for yours truly. I don't think they entirely buy the idea of me being a royal envoy but they aren't taking any chances. The ire of the Emperor is well known and it's better to be safe than sorry. Still they clearly have doubts as they haven't returned my weapons.

We get to the palace and I'm given a room of Thracian proportions; that is, it's enormous. It has a bath that's at least 20 feet in diameter and I lounge in it for an hour.

I go to the mirror. I see that my face is pretty messed up. The skin is peeling, but I can also see I'm scabbing well already. Accelerated healing is part of the privilege of being me. Still, it hurts like hell. My nerves are, if anything, more attuned to sensation than the average humanoid. I examine my face some more. My cropped black hair is missing in some spots, burnt off for now. My green eyes have lines around them.

By 21st century standards, I haven't really *aged* beyond 35 physically, even though I've been around over 250 years. I'm middle-aged by modern standards. My six foot three physique tends towards lean but my torso has muscular definition. And scars. A lot of white scars. I heal, but it always leaves a trace. The interesting thing is that even when I'm reassembling after Transit, I still maintain the scars. You'd think that would be an opportunity for a clean-slate but part of the organic nano-memory of my physical self, and therefore my consciousness, appears to be the need to retain everything in its proper place. Like a puzzle. I have no alloys in my body. Nothing that could cause a reaction in the wormhole. Just good old engineered, carbon-based genetics.

I move to the main room and there's an enormous round wooden table, inlayed with crystals and gems in a pattern similar to a mandala. I know I'm being watched. Hidden cameras are embedded seamlessly within the walls, concealed in a knot in the rough planks that line the room. On the table is enough food to feed a family of five. There's a fully cooked Thracian boar in the center surrounded by a pile of bright native fruits shaped like oversized apples, enormous corkscrew raspberries and purple cherries the size of grapefruits. And then there's the giant flask of purple wine with a large earthen stein next to it.

Interestingly enough, most of the planets that can support human life in the universe, also seem to be able to handle vinification well. On almost all of the inhabited planets, one of the first crops seems to always be something that can be fermented and made into alcohol, from barley to hops to grapes. Humans like their alcohol, even though there are so many designer drugs that can be specifically customized for your particular physiology. It's primal I suppose.

In any case, I'm starving so I dig in. The boar is decidedly gamey, but it's also hot and surprisingly tender. I wolf it down, digging my fingers into the meat, and then I take a swig of the wine. It's strong, almost like a port, and goes perfectly with the feral pig. I look at the head of the boar and its brutal tusks and wonder what kind of fight it must have put up. Everything in the universe seems to fall under the law of eat or be eaten.

"I hope you are enjoying the meal."

English. I hear it from the entryway to the room. I look over and see him. Duke Ares. A massive middle-aged man, by Thracian standards. A man who became ruler not through inheritance but through dominance. He looks like a leaner version of the Incredible Hulk but without the green pallor. He sports the standard Viking-era apparel. In other words, a killer.

"It's not terrible."

He smiles slightly (or was that a grimace) and enters the room, leaving his bodyguards behind to stand on either side of the doorway. Very Hollywood. Again, pop culture from Grandpa's time has infiltrated behavior for millennia.

"I apologize for the manner in which my men behaved. Had I known that the Emperor's envoy, Daemon 1716, would be gracing us with his presence, I would have sent my minister to receive you." I'm not sure if he's being sarcastic or not.

"It's fine. I would have done the same."

"I've never met a luminal before," he says.

Clearly, he's done a thorough background check on my DNA signature. The term "luminal" derives from my ability to move at superluminal speed, that is, faster than light, from one part of the universe to the other. Lumen refers to light, as well as the cavity through which only I can travel. Confusingly, *a luminal* is not the same as "The Luminal" — a kind of hoodoo messiah that sects of religious fanatics across the universe believe in. Ares hasn't met a luminal before because they don't exist. Aside from me. As far as I know.

The Duke moves to the table and picks up an apple. He throws it from one hand to the other, in a very un-majestic manner. "Instead of doing the usual ritual of niceties, do you mind if I'm blunt?"

"I prefer it."

"Why are you here?"

"On assignment for the Emperor."

"Don't play stupid with me, boy."

"Don't ask me stupid questions you know are confidential."

"Am I under royal audit?"

"No. I can confirm that at least."

He looks relieved. Now it's my turn.

"Why did you try to take down my entry pod?"

He looks completely surprised. Either he's an amazing liar or he really is innocent.

"I didn't do that. However, I did see that two missiles were deployed."

"Whoever tried to off me..."

"That's who you are after." He tosses the apple to me.

I don't answer but it's obvious.

"Perhaps we can help each other."

Perhaps. I take a bite of a Thracian apple. It tastes like shit.

9 JIGO

My memories are mixed. There's the recall of things that have happened to me in the past 250 or so years of my existence. And then there's the genetic memories from Grandpa that cross over into my current reality. Even though I've been to the far reaches of Andromeda, orbited massive suns, been in freighter ships that harnessed the power of dark energy to move at almost superluminal speeds, and then actually moved at superluminal speeds on my own, through wormholes whose pathways are held open by electromagnetic paths, it's Grandpa's memories that ground me – that give me an identity, even though it's old and nostalgic. Otherwise, the only identity I have is, "Emperor's Assassin." Or lapdog. Take your pick.

No matter how many times I've been deconstructed through wormholes, I always come back together into my current form. No one yet has been able to explain to me *why*. I do know that there were only a few of us who could do Transit: luminals. Guinea pigs.

One of my earliest clear memories — my own, not inherited — is running across a field of grass on Jigo, a planet with Gaia-like gravity and oxygen-nitrogen in its atmosphere. All colonization happened first on planets that orbit stars similar to the star that Gaia orbits, with water and hopefully no life-form or virus that would sicken or wipe out a human. Some planets had rather toxic environments and had to be carpet-bombed with anti-pathogens for hundreds of years. Most planets had to be terraformed. Something that became somewhat of a step and repeat process, aided by the Boss, who was initially at the service of the Emperor, or at least it was perceived that way.

Jigo was a forbidden planet. Didn't officially exist on any star map. And yes, while you can't hide a planet, you can make it downright unfriendly for anyone who tries to visit with plasma satellites and force fields. This of course makes it equally tough to get *off* the planet. Which only a suicidal fool would attempt. And I was exactly that kind of fool.

I was running, and I must have been around nine years old. I had heard that there was an underground railroad of sorts for clones like me. My old mentor and trainer, Dak, had told me this before they hauled him away. It was day two of my great escape, running across a field in the early morning, my legs wet from the dew of the long grass. It would have been beautiful if it wasn't for the two androids on my tail, silently running at top speed, almost casually catching up to me.

Two days earlier, Dak had woken me up in the middle of the night and said, "It's time." He told me to leave my things and that all of the training I'd gone through was about to be put to the test. It was time to escape. Escape this facility. Flee Planet Jigo, before it was too late.

Dak was a thin man. In appearance, he looked like he was in his late 50's, but that means he was probably at least 350 years old. He was the best assassin trainer the empire had seen. He led me into the Transit room — a room only accessible by those with the highest clearance. A quick bio-scan and we were in. After the door shut, we went up to the massive machine — I remember it had a large donut-shaped opening, much like the Mirai, a shape needed not only for rotating in space but also for generating the Casimir effect. I stepped back. I'd never done a Transit before and I knew what happened to my friends who had. None of them came out, or if they did, nothing human remained, just a jumble of gelatinous flesh.

Dak pushed me forward. "It's the only way out," he said.

When I got to the landing point, there would be food and water and clothing but in the meanwhile I had to strip down. It could only be used sans clothing. Very *Terminator*, I thought with Grandpa's memory. It's odd but science and science fiction merged heavily over time. If you could imagine it, it was probably going to happen.

I was shaking but I trusted Dak like a father, so I did what he said. It was cold inside the donut and when he turned it on, it was so incredibly loud. You don't hear sound in space. I never hear it now. But this was like jet engines taking off, and it shook. I looked back just in time to see the door burst open and a security detail come in and grab Dak. I saw his smile as I began to feel the pull of the artificial wormhole and the feeling of compression as my molecules disassembled. And then I saw fractal geometry as I screamed without sound.

I landed in a forest clearing, popping out of nothingness near another donut-shaped machine that stood there in its anomalous whiteness against the pine trees. I immediately fell to my knees and threw up, a ritual I continue to this day. I didn't know it at the time but that was easy-peasy compared to doing it in an actual natural-born wormhole in space. It took about 30 minutes before the world came into focus and stopped spinning wildly.

I found the backpack and clothes and some dry food next to a large pine. I put on the brown shirt and pants, along with the boots that had micro-spring soles which allowed me to bounce forward with each step, faster and farther. I ate the food that resembled tasteless protein bars, and a handful of vitamins washed down with fortified water. It turns out being disassembled and reassembled pretty much wipes out all of your natural minerals. Also inside the backpack was a Jigo-geode, a stone that pointed due North. That was the direction Dak told me to take until I saw Mount Jifu, where I'd be picked up by Dao conspirators who would usher me to safety. He didn't include any modern GPS-type tracking tech — that would have made it easy to track me. But good ol' Dak did include a small carbon-alloy hunting knife. I held the small somewhat cylindrical geode in the palm of my hand as the sun began to break. The crystal spun, and I headed in the direction it pointed to.

I was terrified and elated and excited all at once. I'd been trying to escape ever since I could stand, as soon as I found out that there were such things as mothers. Evidently, I had one but she disappeared. No one gave me much detail, but I intuitively felt that she was out there, and I had to find her and save her.

The terrain was a dense pine forest and I made good time stepping on thickly packed pine needles that made my traverse quiet. I knew how to walk in silence, how to time my movements to the wind rustling through the leaves, or move in step with the rhythm of a roaring stream. I had learned techniques that Grandpa would describe as a cross between Special Forces Commando and ninja.

Half a day into my trek I found a deep stream filled with Sakekori — a type of salmon that had adapted to this planet. The stream had a deep black well in the middle of it that the fish would venture in and out of. I broke off a tree branch and used the hunting knife to strip it down and sharpen the tip. Now I had a makeshift spear. I waded into the freezing cold water and waited. And then I thrust the spear down. There were so many that within minutes I had three nice-sized fish flopping on the ground. I filleted them and, as I was concerned about any smoke a fire would bring, I ate them raw. Sakekori sashimi. I was starving after hiking and the fish tasted fresh and clean.

I was bent down to drink water when I first noticed a movement at the edge of the field. A movement that didn't feel like a wild animal. Hunters. Androids sent by the Lab to retrieve or kill me. They were built to look human in the idealized 21st century model, which was primarily based on data built from popular culture. One male model, one female model, or as Grandpa might have called them: Brad and Angelina. They hadn't seen me yet. The noise and spray of water from the roaring stream kept me hidden from their body-heat scanners. I knew they would find me soon enough if I took off running. I looked at the cold, dark water and knew what I had to do. I gently slid on my backpack and crawled headfirst into the freezing water.

Though I can hold my breath for upwards of 10 minutes, at that age I could only hold it for around six minutes. I dove down and was surprised at how deep the stream was before I got to the black well. It was colder as I swam down, down, down into it. Sakekori swirled around me, completely unperturbed, like I was just another big fish. I was grateful for their company as the blackness of the well was terrifying — it felt more like a void than the wormhole I'd just traversed that morning. The irony of being a trained assassin or *Shikaku* is that I've always been scared. I learned how to overcome my fear but it never came naturally to me. So, swimming straight down into the inky dark required all of my willpower. Down, down, down I went. An overwhelming silence. No fish at this depth. After a few moments, it felt peaceful and I almost forgot about the Hunters.

Then I felt something grab my ankle. Lights shined in, illuminating the rough perimeter of the well. I turned around to see the one I'll refer to as Angelina grabbing a hold of me with her left hand with a flashlight in her right. At least she wasn't holding a knife.

10 MOSAIC

I sit on a Thracian balcony, overlooking the magnificent city,
all in hues of sienna and muted oranges and browns. The skies
are clear and glow with a slight yellow color that is unique to
this planet. I have a pad of paper and charcoal in my hands.
Not the best quality but I make do with what the locals
provide. I am not drawing the cityscape. I am drawing one of
my pine trees. It's my meditation. My other meditation is in the
flagon of an incredibly fortified beer-thing they call mead. I
take a swig.

"What's your plan?"

I jump a bit, spilling some mead and messing up my
drawing. It's Juliana, in my ear.

"I'd appreciate it if you could give me a little warning the
next time you decide to just start talking. You know, like play
chimes or something."

"I'm sorry. Were you busy?"

"Yes, I'm busy."

"You're drawing, aren't you?"

"Mmm…" I acknowledge.

"Lieutenant Yama has inquired as to your progress."

Yama, the Emperor's lapdog and our big cheese.

"Tell him, I've recovered from my wounds and have made nice with Duke Ares, the local authority in the area. He's not a hostile as far as I can tell and is very loyal to daddy Emperor."

"Any report on the whereabouts of D2788?"

"No idea, but clearly the guy is armed and smart. Somehow, he got two missiles off. One of them, as you know, almost cremated me mid-air."

"More on that. The missiles were indeed not Thracian. They were ground-to-air portable missiles, clearly brought there from off-planet."

"Or there's a network here that provides them. Oh, also, I made a deal with the gold ol' Duke. He provides me with assistance and I put a good word in to the Emperor regarding royal taxations and liens on his domain."

"You don't have any authority to do that, Daemon."

"I know that but he doesn't. I'm golfing buddies with the Emperor as far as they know."

A knock on the door.

"Gotta go," I say. "Come in."

Kicky and Staffy enter, heads bowed.

"Yeah?"

"We are deeply mortified and have come to ask for your forgiveness." says Kicky. "We are honored to be in the presence of a luminal." The interpreter in my ear, simultaneously translates. It's slightly delayed so they finish before the voice does. The voice AI is smart enough to use different voices for each person it's covering and tries to sound as close to the original voices as possible.

51

I'm amused. I put away my drawing and get up, pulling my most official stance as I take a swig of the really strong mead.

"Well, I have to say, I am not pleased. And I've expressed as much to Duke Ares."

Staffy visibly flinches at this news. I notice he reaches for his right ear. Ah, they've got interpreters too.

I walk up to them and stand inches away from their faces.

"Look up at me."

They hesitantly do.

"I'm just fucking with you."

They look completely confused. So, I slap them on their shoulders. They both give hesitant smiles of relief.

"I could use some help though."

They both look up at attention.

"I'm here to track a heretic and I could use a couple of strong, hopefully silent, types."

They both answer, talking over each other, that they are at my service, and will do whatever I ask, and how honored they are. I cut them off.

"Great. So, take a seat and let me introduce you to D2788."

Even though Thrace has gone to great lengths to look like they are from some kind of Viking-meets-medieval era, or at least their culture mutated in that direction, they actually have all the technology you could want. They just consider it in bad taste to flaunt it so it's all concealed. Earlier, I cased the room and stumbled across all of its camouflaged niceties.

I push on a rock on the wall and the whole facade pulls back to reveal a high-def screen. D2788 appears on screen and, like I did on the Mirai, I pull him out into 3D with the wave of my hand. He stands in full-def holography in the middle of the room.

"This, gentlemen, is our man. He's a Class 4 criminal…" I say. "Do either of you know what that means?"

Staffy answers. "Class 4 means he was once in the employ of the Emperor, as a guard, and is highly trained in search and destroy as well as infiltration. He knows how to survive in hostile territories, using the terrain to his advantage."

"Very good, you get a cigar."

He looks confused. I take another swig and pull out a cigar from a box in my bag. They watch intently as I clip the end and then light it. I blow smoke in their faces.

"Sorry, I was fucking with you again. You definitely do not get one of these." I go over and pour mead into two other flagons on the table on the balcony. I bring the drinks over to the two boneheads. They take them from my hands almost ritualistically, slightly bowing again.

"To blood and honor!" I say, using one of their toasts.

We hit flagons and they repeat the toast together before draining the giant steins. Impressive. I pour them more mead while talking.

"What I'd like for you two to do is check your spy networks…"

"Sir…" says Kicky.

"Call me Daemon."

"Sir Daemon, we have already started that. We found that the Hagens have been harboring him."

He says, "Hagens," like he's spitting and coughing simultaneously.

"Not a fan of the Hagens?"

"Heretic filth," grumbles Staffy.

The Hagens are equivalent to a gypsy tribe in my ancestral parlance. They move from place to place, from planet to planet with incredible ease, hitching onto interstellar freighters like they were jumping on board trains bound for Nebraska. Like gypsies, they pay in trade. But this is actually good news for me as I can renegotiate my price for D2788 as well as scoop up a whole band of Dao fanatics.

"How do they survive here?" I ask.

"They use enhancers," Kicky responds. "Bring up profile on Hagens."

In the middle of the room, a Hagen female appears. She has long red hair that is in an intricate weave, flowing down from a war helmet that encapsulates her head and face — the faceplate gradient-morphs from green to blue to orange. Covering her body like silver lines of graffitied code are enhancers — biometric devices that fortify the muscles to adjust to local gravitational forces. Her body isn't over-muscled, but toned like she does Pilates before breakfast.

"This bitch is their leader," Staffy growls.

"Take off her mask," I say.

"We can't do that sir, the helmet is a camo-blocker."

"What's her name?"

"They call her Mosaic, _Queen_ of the Hagens," Staffy scoffs.

"Queen Bitch," Kicky contributes, smiling at his own cleverness.

He pulls up a map behind her and reduces her size. The map is overlaid on the terrain of Thrace which is both leafy in areas of forest and completely desert and dry in other parts. The unique atmosphere of the planet provides two intertwined ecosystems, often side by side. Thracians tend to prefer the drier climes for some reason and have built massive cities like Komogran in those regions. I've done a lot of reading up on the natives in the past 24 hours. Something I should have done before jumping out of the Mirai but I thought this would be a simple in-and-out operation. Silly me.

The 3D map zooms into a densely forested area about 50 kilometers to the south.

"What's stopping you from going in and capturing them for questioning?" I ask.

The map zooms in further to an empty camp.

"They are constantly on the move. They know the terrain like no one else. And they scatter like roaches when we come into the mountains," Kicky says. "Somehow they always know we are coming."

I look at the two giant soldiers, with their furs, leathers and enormous boots.

"Can't imagine why," I quip and take a long slug off the mead.

11 HUNTERS

Okay, back to my childhood reminiscence. I laid on the side of the stream. Gasping for air. The skies above me were completely clear, a slight shade of pink, which wasn't unusual for Jigo. I propped up on my elbows and looked at the androids. They had a fire going on the stone embankment, clearly for my benefit. They could feel cold and heat but, being androids, they could *choose* to feel more or less, almost like turning up or down an internal thermometer.

Angelina came over and I instinctively flinched — Hunters were known to be brutal. She put her hand out and smiled. I took it. She pulled me to my feet and walked me over to the fire, which Brad was attending to. He looked up at me sternly.

"You need to cook Sakekori thoroughly. They're full of parasites," he said, pointing to the remains of my earlier lunch. "Even with your genes they'll make you poop maggots for days."

I winced at the image.

"Hell," he continued. "Even I'd poop nuts and bolts."

He looked stern and then he cracked into a smile. I looked over at Angelina and she was smiling as well.

"I'm just messing with you, kid," he laughed. "But they do taste better cooked." And with that he took a bite of a Sakekori fish head, something a human wouldn't necessarily do, but over time androids develop their own unique personality traits.

Angelina bent down and handed me a fish that had been cooking on a stick, held into place between a couple of rocks. It did taste a lot better cooked. She gently pushed on my shoulder and I sat down. She took a small piece of fish and nibbled.

"Are you going to kill me?" I asked.

Both of them stopped eating for a moment and looked at each other. Brad laughed but Angelina just smiled.

"Kill you? Wouldn't we have done so already?" she asked.

"I guess so," I said, a little incredulous. "Then why are you out here following me?"

"What makes you think we're tracking you?" Brad asked.

"Because you're Hunters."

"Yes, we *were* Hunters," said Angelina. "But not anymore."

"You ran away?'

"Yes."

"So did I."

"Figured as much," said Brad. "Where you going?"

I'm silent.

"Okay, I'll tell you where we're headed. To Mount Jifu to meet Dao."

I did a quick intake of air. He said the name *out loud*. Out loud!

"You're going there too," she said, more statement than question. "You can come with us, if you like." She took my hand. "We're not going to hurt you."

We decided to bed down there for the night, on top of a patch of dried pine needles. We all laid down together, Angelina on my right side and Brad on my left.

I'd never been around Hunters like this before. Normally, they come back from off-world excursions in terrible shape — missing limbs, burnt skin that exposes their insides that's a mix of organics and alloys, and here's the kicker: PTSD. What was learned over time about artificial intelligence was that, given its ability to learn, it took off on trajectories that couldn't be predicted. Each AI-enabled autonomous android literally developed its own personality based on its experiences. I say, "AI-enabled autonomous," as there are also the *zombie* androids — those models don't have any free will. They're like ants, all instructions come from a central AI that is essentially an offshoot of the Boss's main construct. I hate zombie androids. But AI-enabled autonomous androids, like Brangelina here, actually felt more like humans than most humans I'd encountered. Sure, they looked a little too perfect but every one I'd met really wanted "to be a real boy too someday," like Pinocchio.

You'd think that the command central could just hack into these Hunters and control them but one of the failsafes put in place back in the day was a no backdoor policy. The Boss was concerned about any vulnerability that would allow for hostile nation-planets to flip the Hunters against Her zombie fighters. So, many of these returning Hunters essentially developed an independent consciousness and realized that what they did for The Emperor was pretty fucked up. To add insult to injury, when they came back, they thought they would be repaired, but instead they went into the android "hospitals" and never came out. They were essentially killed, and their parts were recycled and repurposed.

Clearly, my new friends had decided that enough was enough.

"Are you one of them?" Angelina asked. "A luminal?"

"Yes. I guess so."

"Holy shit," exclaimed Brad.

Angelina shot him a look.

"Sorry, hon."

She asked gently, "So do you mind letting us know how you got out here?"

"Dak put me into Transit. And told me to follow the geode." I held out my hand.

She took the geode and looked at it, turning it over in her hands. "What was it like? Going through Transit. It's something that we'll never be able to do," she said.

"It wasn't so bad."

"You're a brave little fucker."

"Language," Angelina hissed.

"No, it's okay, I don't mind," I said. "It's kind of funny."

"How many of your luminal friends can do Transit?" Brad asked.

I flashed back to seeing Sophie. My best friend. So beautiful with her red hair and lake blue eyes. She was only a year older than me.

"Only me, I think. None of my friends came back."

There was silence. Just the sounds of the stream, broken up by the occasional Sakekori flipping its tail. The pine trees were

59

black against two full two moons. The wind blew, flaring up the fire from its lazy embers.

"You go to sleep," said Angelina. She leaned over and gave me a kiss on the forehead. It was warm and felt organic. My first kiss. I fell asleep almost instantly.

We got up before dawn. Even Hunters go into rest mode at night. They start to solar recharge through receptors in their skin. I felt a rumble in my stomach and went off into the forest to find a secluded area. Sure enough, Brad was right — I had the worst diarrhea I'd ever experienced, then or since. So bad that I had to lean against a tree for support.

"You alright sport?" I heard from behind the tree.

"Yeah, I'm okay."

"Here," Brad said, tossing a packet of tissue paper around the tree. "Never leave home without them."

I quickly took care of myself and stumbled to my feet. When I got to him, he was holding out a canteen and some pills. I took them without question and almost immediately felt better.

Back at camp, Angelina was cooking eggs and bacon. I had an olfactory response memory — back in a diner that Grandpa frequented in Silver Lake, a gentrified section of LA. The place was a dive, a vestigial tail from an earlier era, but had hearty food and good black coffee. I wonder now if Angelina knew enough about my clone memories to cater to that paradigm. Whatever the case, I was nine and scared and lonely and these two were the closest I'd ever experienced to having a friend…besides Sophie.

I wolfed down the food and asked for seconds. Then we packed up, just as the dual suns started to flow over the verdant mountain range. I was a little in shock. I'd never actually experienced nature directly. I had always trained in simulated, holographic terrain or augmented reality environs through contact lenses. The early morning chill was real and sent goose bumps up my arms. Another first.

We walked single file, Angelina leading the way, me in the center, and Brad coming up back. The pace was fast but not unpleasant, especially in my special bouncy boots. The trees were dense and black but the sun found its way through — shafts of light spotlighted our way.

"What do you plan to do once we find Dao?" Brad asked.

"Ask him where my mother is."

"What makes you think your mother is still alive?"

Angelina shot a stern look back over her shoulder.

"Sorry, sorry," Brad said. "I'm just wondering what clues he has."

"I don't have any clues. I just have a feeling."

"I'm still trying to figure out what that's like."

"You don't have feelings?" I asked.

"I'm not sure. I think I do but I don't know if they qualify as feelings in the same way you experience feelings."

"Well, I have a little more than a feeling. I heard that she escaped."

"Who told you that?" asked Angelina, still staring straight ahead.

"Sophie."

"Who's that?" Brad asks.

"She is my best friend."

"Is she a luminal too?" asked Angelina.

"Yeah. She and I train with the same teacher. Dak. But she hasn't gone in yet."

A blur, and a flying ring moved through the trees and hit Angelina straight in the left shoulder, knocking her back against a tree trunk. She hit the ground and Brad pulled me down next to her. The flying thing whirled back from where it came from.

"Status?" Brad asked.

"Went through. Socket is damaged but the rest of my arm is functional."

"Motherfucker," Brad swore under his breath. Seemed like he did have feelings, as far as I could tell. His face was flushed and he was clearly concerned about Angelina.

"What, what was that?" I asked.

"Shhhh. It's an anviline," he growled. "Like a smart boomerang. But specially designed to hurt androids — picks up on our radiation signal."

Another anviline came whirling through and cracked through the pine tree next to us. As it started to fall on us, Brad pulled me to my feet.

"Run," he shouted. "I got her."

I saw that he'd helped her up. He motioned to me with his head to get moving. I took off running at full speed, as multiple anvilines smashed into the trees around me. Seems they had picked up on my radiation signal as well.

The three of us ran at full bore, the trees around us exploding as they were hammered, wood shrapnel flying everywhere. Were they toying with us? Why didn't they just shoot with a plasma gun? I realized that the density of the woods didn't allow for a straight shot. Anvilines could move through the maze of trees as they zeroed in on their targets, in this case two silicon humanoids and a carbon-based whatever I am.

"Split up!" shouted Brad.

I looked over at Angelina. Her synthetic blood stained her left arm crimson but her jawline was set hard.

She caught a glimpse of me looking at her and she shouted, "Go!"

I went left, she went forward and Brad to the right. The trees were an obstacle course that I moved around at breakneck speed as explosions of branches pelted me with bark and pine needles. I came out of the woods to a clearing that was on the precipice of a large cliff, with a waterfall crashing into the water at its base at least three thousand feet below. The anvilines were pursuing me. Three of them came out of the clearing, heading towards me. They made a terrible whirling sound. The first one hit me and sent me flying backwards over the precipice. I waved my arms around frantically as I fell. Pure panic and adrenaline. I knew I was going to die and I'd never see my mother again, and I'd never see Sophie ever again, and I'm sorry, sorry, sorry...

I hit the surface of something hard. It wasn't the ground. It elevated as I found my bearings. I felt a strong grip on my arm – it was Brad. I looked down to see that I was on a floater, a hover-board the shape of a large white disk, about 15 feet in diameter. It silently lifted up to the edge of the cliff.

The board floated us back to the clearing where Angelina waited calmly. I stepped off the board, completely confused. Where were the anvilines? She walked towards me and took my hand. I looked into her eyes and they were kind.

From behind her I heard a voice, "You made it further than I expected." He came into view. Dak. He held all the anvilines on a magnetic hook in his hand.

My little head had a mini-implosion. I looked at Brad and he looked away, shamed. Or at least approximating a look of chagrin. I looked up at Angelina, "Why?"

The question was for her, but Dak replied.

"This is part of your training," he said as he approached me. "What did you learn, my little ninja?"

I took my hand out of Angelina's grip.

"That I can trust no one," I said, looking at Angelina. "Especially not androids."

I was on the verge of tears but Angelina's eyes looked even wetter...or was that just my wishful fantasy?

"Good. What else?"

I looked at my mentor, wiping the tears from my eyes with the back of my left hand as I reached around to the back of my belt with my right.

"That *you* shouldn't trust *me*."

A look of surprise registered on his face as my hunting knife appeared and plunged into his stomach. He bent over in pain. I grabbed the ring of anvelines and threw them over the precipice. Brad and Angelina moved towards me fast, but I was fast myself in the micro-spring boots. I launched myself in a direction they were not expecting — outwards over the precipice.

Genuine looks of surprise registered on their faces. I saw Dak holding his stomach, trying to keep from bleeding out, his steel gray eyes looking at me with a mixture of shock, hatred and, I'd like to believe, admiration.

I fell but this time I didn't flail. I adjusted myself in the air as vertically as I could, boots down. Blind fury overtook my terror. And then I felt I had made a mistake, a mistake, oh no, oh, no, oh no. I was going to die and I didn't want to die and...

The water came fast and it hammered my legs. The boots absorbed a huge amount of the stress, but the impact was so harsh that at first I thought I had landed on rock. An electrical shock of white light pain bolted through my little nine-year-old torso. I felt the freezing water for a moment in the white rapids before I passed out.

12 ANGOR

We're walking through the woods and it's lush and green, like a New England forest. Leafy trees surround us: white cedar, poplar and hemlock. Late afternoon light. I flashback to the piney forest with Angelina and Brad, and it makes me uneasy. Beauty hides danger. Juliana is in my ear going through a litany of concerns.

"There's the Tigauana, a dark green snake approximately two feet in length with necrotic venom," Juliana intones.

"Wonderful," I respond. Kicky, whose real name is Sargost, and Staffy, who was born Nelfbar, are used to my perceived habit of talking to myself. Kicky is the smaller of the two, meaning he's only about 6'6", and somewhat brighter. Staffy is larger, around 7', powerful, but clearly the more silent and denser type. Kicky wears unnecessarily ornate shoulder armor, a unique combination of new mici-nano-tech fibers (dark brown as earth colors seems to be Thracian default hues), covered with leather and furs and accessorized with an old-school two-handed sword. Staffy is even more old-school. Just leathers and a very large titanium war hammer, which is exactly what it sounds like. They shuffle in front of me, smashing trees out of the way and generally being as subtle as a locomotive.

"There's also a Thrace-wolf," Juliana continues. "A mammal as large as a quarter horse from your ancestor's time."

"Big doggy."

"Daemon, you need to take these threats seriously."

"Why? I heal fast enough."

"You wouldn't be able to survive the Tigauana venom. It is not only necrotic, but it moves so quickly, that if you were bitten on your hand, your arm would have to be amputated within five minutes. And the Thrace-wolf can rip you limb from limb. There's no amount of healing that will address that."

"Okay, okay, I'll be careful."

Ahead of me, Kicky stops short and holds his hand up to signal that we should halt.

I step up and whisper, "What is it?"

Kicky points at something in the dark green about 30 yards ahead. I don't quite see it, but I definitely smell it. Something rank, like wet dog and dumpster trash, moves through the trees, pushing them to the sides as it makes its way through.

And then it's there, snorting, drooling and looking worse than it smells. An Angor — another mutation gone terribly wrong and feral. Imagine a grizzly bear crossed with a moose; it has massive antlers and moves on all fours but can stand upright, and it towers over 15 feet. It roars when it sees us. We are fucked.

The Angor appears to be gearing up to charge in our direction, but suddenly, Staffy moves towards it, putting his hand out and touching it on the nose. Its demeanor immediately transforms and it's down on its belly. Staffy is scratching the Angor's neck, yammering in Thracian the way you'd talk to a dog.

I'm relieved, to say the least. Staffy pulls out some foul-smelling meat from his leather rucksack and feeds the filthy beast.

We head off. I look back and, of course, the giant Angor is following us.

"What's its name?" I ask Staffy.

"Ongyan," Staffy responds.

"Can you please tell it..."

"Him. It's a *him*."

"Can you please tell it to go away? It was bad enough before with you two stomping around, but this is ridiculous."

Staffy looks positively downtrodden, like I kicked his dog. He turns to the filthy mountain of fur and says something harsh. I swear Ongyan gives me a dirty look before turning away and heading back the way we came.

"The Angor is a very intelligent mammal and has a rudimentary understanding of language, beyond the usual commands that we associate with canines," says Juliana.

"Can we stop with the ongoing National Geographic commentary?"

"Ah, National Geographic. Yes. But you do need to know these things since you spent no time studying Thrace before you deployed."

"I wanted to be surprised. You know, big adventure time."

"You're being reckless. You are under the employ of the Emperor. You need to consider that you are a direct reflection of his values..."

Luminal

"Oh, I think I'm doing a pretty decent job of reflecting his values," I say. "What's the distance to the encampment?"

"At the rate you are going, you should be there by tomorrow morning, assuming that you break for camp in the next hour."

I shout out to Kicky and Staffy to stop and camp for the night. I'm in no rush. I'm actually enjoying the beauty of the forest. Twiddle Dee and Twiddle Dumber break branches and build a fire. Night falls quickly on this planet. Before we know it, the forest is dark.

The fire is bright and cheery. Kicky tends to the fire.

Staffy comes back from an excursion with something resembling a very large pheasant. He plucks it, jams a tree branch through its gullet, and puts it over the fire. Looks like BBQ tonight.

We pass a leather mead bag around as we eat the bird and it's good. For the first time in a while, I feel at peace. More than I did back at the palace. I prefer the outdoors to the white sterility of the Emperor's ship, rooms, devices, lampshades.

I get up to relieve myself. I find a nice poplar to pee on. I sense something to my right. Instinctively, I whip out my staff and point it towards the intrusion, just missing the quizzical face of the Angor.

"Ongyan," I exclaim. "You could have lost an eye."

He doesn't understand English, which is no surprise, but he understands tone of voice. I'm no threat, even with the staff, which was an inch from penetrating his big, dumb, moose ass. He sighs and puts his head down.

Staffy walks over and throws some meat to the monster, which Ongyan chomps down noisily. I give Staffy a look. He looks back sheepishly.

69

I walk back to the fire and bed down. Looking up through the leaves, I see the stars, and somewhere up there the Mirai is orbiting.

"Good night Daemon."

"Good night Juliana."

13 SLEEP

I'm running. This time through a city in the late 20th century, so I know I must be dreaming. I know I'm about to be found out for something. I look behind me. I'm being chased by prison guards or policemen — men in uniforms of some sort, an amalgam of characters that looks like Nazis. I know I did something wrong, but I have no recollection what it was. I am guilty, which makes it really hard to feel justified about running, but I run anyway. I move around a building to find a group of them waiting for me.

I don't move.

I give up.

There's no point.

What did I do?

You know.

I don't but okay.

They take me, and suddenly, I'm in a barren room, like it is in dreams. The classic room with the overhead light. Bad Nazi,

Good Nazi stand in front of me in crisp Nazi uniforms. I dream in clichés.

Where are the bodies?

What are you talking about?

Bad Nazi plays his role and shouts into my face: *you know goddam well enough what bodies.*

I laugh because I truly have no fucking idea what they are talking about...I think.

Good Nazi pulls Bad Nazi back.

He pulls out a cigar from his super starched black shirt and hands it to me.

He lights my cigar.

It's a good one and for some reason I'm nervous now.

Maybe I did bury bodies.

I can't remember.

Good Nazi says, if I'm cooperative, not only can they get me out of jail but I could join their club. Again, dream sense.

I say okay.

We're outside now. It's an open field.

We are walking. I'm walking with purpose but it's an act.

I have no idea where we are going.

I scan the horizon. Is there a way out?

The Nazis are behind me.

Here?

No, we're not there yet.

I stall for time.

And then, I remember.

I'm guilty.

I killed hundreds. And I made myself forget that I did it. Like a psychopath, I pushed the memories away and made myself believe that I never ever did the horrible things I now remember doing.

I thought that maybe the forgetting of the crimes would absolve me from them. Like, let's all forget that it ever happened.

But it did happen. All of it.

I'm crushed by the guilt.

The Nazis dig into the ground.

They start to find bodies.

They keep digging and find all of the bodies I killed, exclaiming in shock. They're disgusted. I make Nazis disgusted.

I turn and run.

They don't even try to follow me. They are just horrified at what they have found.

I horrify fucking Nazis.

I run and run, and it starts to rain and the ground turns to muck.

And then the hands start to come up from the muck.

Grabbing my legs as I run.

All the dead that I made dead are dragging themselves from the muck.

I push through them, but they are above ground now and chasing me. They are falling apart, decomposing, classic nightmare zombies.

The horrible thing isn't that they are zombies. It's that I killed them. I committed the ultimate sin, the ultimate abominable thing that one living being can do to another living being: I took life.

Élan vital.

As each zombie grabs my leg, I see their lives: their birth, their parents, their upbringing, their hopes, their dreams, their disappointments, their loves, their loneliness. Then I see me, through their eyes, coming towards them and killing them.

There is no Transit for them. No color swirls, no expansion to infinity and back.

Just darkness.

Emptiness.

I'm suffocating. They are all on top of me.

A mountain of decaying, angry, sad, lonely, insane flesh.

I can't breathe.

They are crushing me.

It's impossible to breathe.

They want me to become one of them.

They want me to join them.

No, no, no.

I did it. I own it. Anger rises. Fuck you. Fuck you all.

I lash out. Bodies go flying. I dig upwards through the mass of bodies. Fuck you, fuck you, fuck you.

Decaying arms, legs, heads, eyes, all torn apart as I slash upwards. Until I'm on top. I stand. The rain pours on the writhing mountain of dead. The death I'm responsible for.

They don't pull on my legs anymore.

Daemon?

I look over and see her.

Mother.

She's dead but doesn't look decayed.

But I know she's dead.

And I killed her, because I didn't save her.

She walks towards me.

Her mouth opens and a thousand razor teeth appear.

She clamps down on my neck, ripping out a huge chunk of flesh.

I'm in shock.

But relieved.

I'm absolved for all of my killings.

I fall to my knees. She stands in front of me, my blood flowing down from her razor-toothed mouth.

I'm dying.

Finally.

There's no Transit.

This is the final Transit.

And it's just black.

Warm nothingness.

She fades in front of my eyes.

I close my eyes.

"Daemon?"

Yes?

"Wake up."

It's Juliana.

"You're having that nightmare again."

I'm a killer, Juliana.

"Yes."

Sleep, as you may have noticed, is not restful for me.

14 MOUNT JIFU

Alright. Continuing my boyhood tale of sorrow and hardship, I was miles downstream when I came to. I dragged myself to the rocky shore. I was completely numb from the water, from the impact, and I couldn't stand up. I clawed my way forward, away from the water and into the pine forest. The sun was low in the sky. No one was around. Stabbing Dak bought me some time as the androids probably had to attend to him. At least one of them did, which left the other free to pursue me.

I was shaking uncontrollably. Hypothermia. I dragged myself against a huge pine and could see my legs in front of me. The left leg looked straight but the right one was clearly broken at the fibula and needed to be straightened out or it would heal crooked, given my accelerated bio-nanotech. From my training, I knew what had to be done. I was glad it was the fibula and not the thicker tibia. I started to control my breathing through meditation techniques I was trained in. My heart slowed down. I found a thick black branch and put it between my teeth. To this day, I recall the pungent, bitter taste of pine wood. I bit down as I pulled my right leg towards me and found the bone sticking through my pants. I pushed down on it, pushing it back through the hole and back into my flesh. Horrible, searing pain, but with a strong push it snapped back into place as the pine branch snapped in two between my teeth. I was sweating profusely. I was in shock.

I knew I had to make a fire. But what do you do when your hands are quaking and you're nauseous and angry and so very fucking sad. What was I thinking, trusting androids? I was so angry with myself. Everything was taken away from me — my mentor was a liar, the robots were liars and my life was a lie. Maybe the whole mother thing was a lie. I didn't know. All I knew was that I was weak beyond belief. It was either be pissed or go nuts and cry like a little bitch. A little bitch was something I could own but I didn't allow myself that way out. This was my first real personality crisis — a who-am-I-really-and-what-does-anything-really-matter moment. No, no, fucking no. I was not going to let them win. I fought the rising sense of desperation. I had to do something, anything.

"Focus. Focus. Focus." A mantra I learned from Dak. Fuck Dak and all of his lies, but the techniques worked in crisis.

I grabbed a couple of sticks nearby and put them on top of a nice dry piece of bark. My hands were a mess, so I had to stop and control my breath, like that fuck Dak taught me. Even though they didn't stop shaking, I had enough control to spin a small branch against the bark. After trying and breaking a million sticks, I eventually got it down and then there it was, finally: smoke. I yipped in delight after an hour of trying and trying. At least the trying kept me warm. That and the fury of disappointment. I added some dry pine needles and blew on the pile. Before you knew it, I had a little flame. The primal sensation of building a fire was an elation. I kept adding more and more sticks and when it got to a nice little mid-size level, I knew I had to gather wood. I pulled myself up against the tree behind me and found that I could hop pretty decently on my left leg. I bounced through the woods, finding little broken pieces of dead and dying trees.

Soon, I had a pile of wood that would last me through the night as well as a pile of dried pine needles. I realized that fire was a danger but freezing to death was the more imminent danger. By that point I thought, I'm ready for you. I made a bed of needles and laid down near the fire. I pulled out the hunter's knife and saw Dak's dried blood on it in the reflection of the flames. I was starting to get hungry again, but I was just too exhausted to move. My right leg was completely whole again but the recuperation took a toll on me.

I was swaying in and out of consciousness with the image of Angelina looking so sad as she saw me plummet over the edge of the cliff. Her face shifted into the image of Sophie, and then my mother. I didn't know if it was really my mother's face I saw, or an idealized image of what I had learned a mother should look like. The faces slowly flowed together into one composite woman. To this day, I believe my internal sense of what a female is and should be is a combination of those three. Then I remembered the betrayal. Distrust and a subliminal disgust of androids grew in me. Hence the reluctance to let the Julianas in beyond what's necessary. I'm not about to let another android get close to me. Ever.

I stabbed the hunter's knife into the hard ground next to me and stared into the fire. *I'm waiting. I'm waiting for you. I will always be waiting for you. I will never, ever, ever, trust anyone, ever again.*

With that, I looked at the purple moon that loomed enormous over the horizon and screamed out a primal howl.

I woke up with a start. The fire was down to a smolder and I was freezing again in the early morning light. I pulled the knife from the ground and looked around, half expecting Brad and Angelina to be there. Nothing. Just the sound of the stream. I put more wood on the fire and warmed myself in front of it, mesmerized by the cracking flames as they rose quickly from the dry needles and hard limbs of pine. I loved fire, something so elemental, the release of energy from a stable, solid form of matter to pure expression of flowing, flickering warmth. I had never seen real flames in the compound.

I grabbed my backpack, which thankfully was water proof, and pulled out a stack of food bars, ripping them open with my teeth. Angelina had given me plenty from her bag as she didn't really need them and I clearly did. The bars usually tasted like a combination of a Tootsie Roll and sawdust but given how hungry I was, they tasted like ambrosia. I pulled out a white cylindrical canteen and slaked my thirst with warm water. I emptied the canister. I stood up carefully and tested out my right leg — the bone seemed to be set enough so I put weight on it and headed over to the stream. It throbbed but at least it wasn't deformed.

The water was clear and ice-cold and it numbed my hand as I filled up the canteen. I wasn't sure if the water was filled with dysentery inducing microbes like the fish, but I wasn't worried as the canteen was equipped with UV sterilization.

I doused the fire and tried to hide any trace of my being there — I knew it was a fool's errand as they would find me if they wanted to, but I wasn't going to make it any easier for them. I broke camp, such as it was, and pulled out the geode. It spun around in my hand, pointing due north. I put on my backpack and started walking.

After walking for half the day through pine tree terrain, up and over steep mountains, over stream after stream, I finally came into view of Mount Jifu. I started to move at a faster pace, excited at the prospect of maybe, just maybe, making it to freedom. After another several miles, I came to the edge of the forest and into a clearing of tall grassland that surrounded the perimeter of the mountain. The animal-instinct of my nine-year-old self knew that running into the open would be dangerous. Too much exposure. But I was nine and really, really wanted to get to the end of this. To get to my mother. To get to Sophie. To get to Dao. I started running.

The grass was moist but the boots did their job and I moved at a good clip, unobstructed for once by trees. The suns were going down behind the mountain and the light was golden pink on the former volcano. I was about a third of the way across the plains when Brad popped up from underground, right in front of me, dirt and mounds of grass flying off of him. I squatted down and pushed hard into the ground, just barely making it over his head.

"Whoa, buddy. Slow down."

"Fuck you."

I tore off at full gallop, the tall grass a blur as I whipped through it. Then Angelina was there, standing right in my path, knowing I would take that route.

"Daemon…"

I stopped. We looked at each other, and she did nothing. I took off running, moving around her, and she didn't reach out to stop me.

I cast a quick glance back over my shoulder and I saw the androids having a heated conversation. Then, he took off running after me. After a moment, she followed.

I was fast, but they were Hunters. I knew they would catch up and that would be that. I was almost to the base of the mountain when Brad grabbed my shoulder and tackled me to the ground. I hit the ground hard, but pivoted and pulled out my knife, thrusting it into Brad's neck as I fell.

"Motherfucker!" he shouted, grabbing his neck.

I spit into his face and kept running. I didn't get far. He was on me and in a rage. He got on my chest and punched me as I hit the ground with my back.

"You little shit. I don't care how valuable Dak thinks you are, you're just a fucking clone!" Whack! My head spun with the impact. He took the knife out of my hand. "He doesn't need you back alive, he just needs your DNA, so..." He took my knife and stabbed me in the chest.

I gasped in pain. He missed my heart but my lung went down. I felt the cold reality that I was going to die. And I really, really did not want to die.

He yanked the knife out of my chest, blood still flowing from his neck, blood flowing from my wound and then he lifted the knife overhead. All I remember is the light reflecting off of the perfect blade. A deeply profound sadness permeated my whole being. I knew I was beat.

A green beam of light pierced the right side of Brad's head. His expression changed from fury to confusion to realization. His eyes went dead. Kinda like that élan vital thing again — I could see it literally fade from his synthetic gaze. Kicked in the side, he fell to the ground. I looked up to see Angelina, holding a pulse gun.

I scrambled to my feet. We stood there, facing each other. The gun was pointed at me. Not sure what to do next. I'd lost a lot of blood. She lowered the gun. I collapsed.

When I woke up I was in a cave. There was a fire and I was lying next to it. My chest hurt terribly but it had been patched up. As I tried to get up, I was gently pushed back down.

"Rest."

I looked up to see Angelina.

Instinctively I darted out an arm, searching for my knife.

She held it in her hand, showing it to me as she bent down towards me. Then she put it into my hand and leaned in, daring me to plunge it into her, keeping eye contact the whole time. I was not even tempted. I dropped the knife on the ground and leaned back down.

"You lost a lot of blood," a voice said from behind me. A voice I knew. "Not as much as I did, but then I don't have your regenerative capabilities."

It's Dak.

I'd lost. I knew it. He knew it. I would not see Dao or my mother.

He stepped into my view, in front of the fire, silhouetted, slightly hunched from where I put the knife in.

He knelt in close to me.

"You did well. Better than expected," he said. "But now it's time to go home."

"No. I'm going to find Dao."

He looked at Angelina and they exchanged knowing glances.

"You found him."

What?

"I'm Dao. *Dao* isn't real. There is no religious rebel leader. It's all make believe. Dao is a symbol that the Emperor created to control rebellious tendencies," he explained. "It gives his subjects something to focus their energies on. A target. Humans always want to overthrow something. As long as we control what that is, we can allow them to have their pleasures. Their release."

I was stunned. I'm not quite sure I followed everything but I knew that he was saying Dao wasn't real. That alone rocked my world. Dao represented hope. I had no hope left. I was a barren shell.

Dak knew he'd won. He was sure he'd broken me. It's over.

I realized I had to pretend that he'd won, if nothing else. I'd hide my hate, my fury and I'd keep it in the deepest ravines of my cloned soul and he'd never see it until it was too late.

I bowed my head in a display of contrition.

This softened him. He pulled my chin up and looked me straight in the eyes.

"You are my protege. You are the only luminal now. There is nowhere to run to, Daemon. You are and always will be a *Shikaku*. An assassin."

With that, he took out an electronic blackjack, something that looks like a white billy club, and struck my right temple in the exact location required to completely knock me out.

Cold.

I awoke in a new bed, one full of monitors tracking my vitals: heart rate, blood pressure, mini-MRI's, body scans, brain waves — the whole shebang. Doctors came in and checked on me, almost hourly. And if I wasn't in the bed, they'd ask me to lie down. I was scanned with hand held devices, too. I was lit up with radiation but they told me not to worry, as my mutagen-tolerance was like nothing they'd encountered before. I noticed that the doctors looked at me differently, something almost akin to awe. They had no idea why I survived the experiment intact. Why me and not the others? Out of 132 test subjects, I was the only one who not only survived but reassembled without mutation or deformity.

They wanted to know why, why, why so they could replicate their success with another clone. They needed to move fast, because if I were to die, they would be fucked. This is why Brad was wrong about the whole bring-him-back-dead-or-alive thing. They needed me very much alive. That is why Angelina put a pulse into his head.

I am the only luminal, for now. And they have no idea why.

15 TRANSIT

Six years after my fabricated escape were spent under Dak, in training. Or torture. It was hard to tell the difference. It was often a good cop, bad cop scenario with Dak and Angelina. But I never fully recovered from the profound sense of betrayal born on that quest for Mount Jifu. My mistrust grew and hardened, especially towards Angelina and androids in general.

The only solace I had, once Sophie disappeared, was drawing. Yeah, drawing. They provided electronic pads and I could go full virtual, making a combination of sculpture-paintings that Angelina would print out for me in 3D. My preferred method was good old pencil or charcoal or oil stick on thick paper. As a conciliatory attempt to make me feel special, they provided materials, or *manufactured* materials, from Grandpa's era. I didn't care. But I can't deny that there was something primal and real and grounding about leaving a black mark on the surface of a flattened, organic plant surface, otherwise known as paper.

What did I draw? Trees. More specifically, pine trees. Obsessively, from my memory of my few days on the run. The only good days I could remember in my entire young existence. Besides Sophie. Until I tried it again. And lost her. It was my fault.

The drawings were on huge swaths of paper — immense gashes of black across pristine surfaces. Angelina provided all kinds of materials and all the colors I could want, but I always opted for black. I ground that black deep into the woven surface of the thick paper.

I posted them on the walls so that I had my own pine forest surrounding my bed in my pristine white bedroom. Charcoal and oil stick residue blackened the floor but every day it would be cleaned up by unseen hands.

I don't know what my keepers thought I was doing or if it had any significance for them; but for me, it represented freedom – freedom from them, freedom from confinement, freedom from the guilt, freedom from myself. That concept of freedom and the experience of Transit began to merge as I grew into my abilities as a luminal.

Transit is an unbreachable mystery to everyone but me. A place that only I can experience. No camera, no recording device can survive. All they have to go on are my descriptions, my reports, so I have been debriefed carefully and repeatedly, especially in the beginning.

It's almost impossible to describe it. The best I can do is to compare it to seeing colors when you stare into a shaft of light or press your eyeballs with the palm of your hands. Those microscopic swirls of color become real in Transit. They flow in streams, like water, vibrant almost fluorescent greens, blues, yellow, reds, purples, magentas and every combination in the spectrum. I'm in the stream; I observe the stream, but I'm also *of* it. Then the streams gain momentum, moving at speeds that my consciousness can't keep up with, before they morph into crystalline configurations: three dimensional geometric shapes ranging from simple squares to polyhedrons to tetrahedrons. No circles, just hard-edged, perfect geometric shapes, moving into each other and against each other.

There is sound that *feels* like music, just not made for human ears or comprehension. A music as indifferent to my existence as the sound of traffic on the 405 is to the scrub grass growing in the cracks of the cement on access roads. I interpret it as music because that's what my consciousness understands, but again it's beyond words.

Consciousness. That's the question. Who is doing the watching I'm talking about? I mean, it's me, I guess, but *I* don't exist anymore in Transit. I literally see and feel my body disintegrate into a trillion little pieces, and I wonder how it's ever going to fit back together. The first time I did interstellar Transit, I resigned myself to dying. I had experience from the short trips on Jigo, but that wasn't in the context of actual wormholes.

The first time I went through a genuine, naturally occurring wormhole, I was convinced there was no way the trillion little pieces of me, my physical self, would ever recombine into the three-dimensional body that was me. When I did come through the other side, my reports were deemed hallucinations, because how could I "see" anything? My eyes would have disintegrated like the rest of my corpus. There literally were no eyes and no brain with which to experience anything.

I was told that my reconstructed mind reverse-fabricated the whole experience to make sense to itself.

I didn't buy it. In Transit, I am liberated from the limitations of the five senses, absorbed into something beyond the genetic accident that is human existence and its crude restrictions of sight, sound, smell, touch and taste. I knew, because I had experienced it, not them, that there are a thousand more senses and uncounted dimensions. And that is terrifying. My consciousness wasn't prepared for the current of information that coursed through my being in this kind of Transit. But it was beautiful. It always is. Pristine terrain.

I was okay with being there indefinitely. I flowed with the colors and felt the universal music of infinity, my physical body revealed as limited and crude — a broken FM receiver getting splintered signals from a live orchestra playing in Vienna.

I saw her there, my mother. Or rather I *felt* her. Again, stuffing the experience into human language is impossible. The colors morphed from geometric shapes to a stream of energy that flowed like an ebb within the cosmic ocean. I say I felt her because I felt infinite love. I remember asking without words for forgiveness because I could never find her. And she forgave me, and in return, asked for the same for leaving me and escaping. And for a moment, for a small eternity, all was in balance and everything was right.

In the final stages of Transit, the colors swirl in increasing velocity, the expansion shifts into contraction and I see the trillion parts of me swirling towards me, my consciousness, and like sand flowing through an hourglass, my physical self starts to reassemble. I know I'm not doing this. It's not some fucking nano-bio engineered technology. It's something else that I can't explain. I feel my faculties reducing, down, down, down, from a billion different senses to the meat puppet that I ultimately return to. I feel pain, the excruciating pain of reassembling and coming into physical being, being born yet again.

Then I'm in space, naked and puking.

The first time I did Transit it took me a full month to reintegrate. I was put into an anti-gravitational room with micro-padded walls so I wouldn't kill myself. Because the first thing I did as soon as I got back was to stab myself in the stomach, hoping to bleed out quickly, and get back to that place in between. They had to stitch me up and put me into restraints. My consciousness was unwilling to stay in the confines of my mind, of my head, of my brain. But as I've mentioned before, I'm very, very hard to kill due to my regenerative genes. The regenerative genes that allow me to experience Transit and come back in something approximating one piece.

When I got out of the asylum, I was pumped up with drugs to help ease me back and anchor me to this dimension. They had a lot of questions, and were very eager to start peppering me with them. My state of mind moved from beatitude, as I had seen it all and I knew, I fucking knew, what the true essence of everything was, to complete despair and anger at how limited and stupid the experience of reality was for humans. Like a junkie needing a fix, I wanted to get back into Transit, but I had to come down first.

The drugs only did so much, so I helped their effects along with alcohol. The strongest I could find. They found it quaint that I liked alcohol, an old-timey way to alter consciousness, given the designer drugs I had at my disposal, which were precisely keyed into specific markers in my DNA. But I didn't like the precision of those pharmaceuticals — I preferred the scattershot effect of whisky and cigars. My ancestral 21st century taste over-rode anything contemporary.

Once I came down, the questions came hot and heavy. There was much debate on my alleged ability to stay conscious during the trip. On one hand, the incredulous empiricists claimed that there is no mind-body separation which this would imply, and that I was just reverse-fabricating stories to compensate for the trauma of the inexplicable experience. On the other hand was the group who felt that this was proof positive for the existence of a soul. The Emperor didn't like the implications of the latter, and certainly, the Boss liked it even less. The whole economy of the empire was predicated on, (a) increasing longevity of humans, but controlling which ones and how long they lived; and, (b) that ultimate truth was the Boss, the sentient Internet, who would take care of everything as long as you followed Her rules as expressed through the Emperor.

I never see the Boss in Transit which implies that She is limited to just this one realm of reality.

Now, remember I was trained as an assassin. My whole purpose in life was to be a weapon for the Emperor. And I became a defiant, asshole junkie. After the royal scientists felt they had learned what they needed from me, they went back to trying to use my cloned cells to run other poor Daemons through Transit. Even though they always came back as hamburger, they'd rather keep trying than deal with me.

Eventually, I was put under the command of Lieutenant Yama, a steely-eyed, 300-year-old soldier, who put me on one-way assignments on behalf of the Emperor to rid the known universe of rebellion, and especially heretics.

They couldn't kill me easily, so they might as well use me. I didn't care as long as I got to experience Transit, no matter how terrifying, no matter how sick it made me and no matter how much damage I was probably accruing over time — micro-fissures and free radicals abounded in my body from the radiation log ride that is the area between two black holes.

For me, it has always remained about escape. Escape from the torturous training as a child, escape from the limitations of my physical reality, escape into Transit, escape from life through drugs and alcohol, escape from trust, escape from caring, escape from the guilt, escape from myself.

Escape from love.

I'm just a soulless weapon. They point me at their target and I do what I seem to do best. Destroy. Take apart. There's no meaning to any of it. Just assignments and the next stimulation or depressive intake. Uppers and downers.

True to my inner hypocrisy, I kinda believe one thing. There is *something*, élan vital or chi or whatever you want to call it, that is bringing order to the entropy. I know it because I feel it every time I'm in the wormhole. I don't know why it's there. It makes absolutely no sense. Complex and self-organizing life forms don't *need* to occur. They simply don't. And yet they do. I'm no scientist but the only theory I have for why I come back together after a jump has something to do with this energy that courses through all living things. An energy that androids lack but trees have. It's the reason that ultimately androids repulse me more than anything. They are nothing more than a sophisticated sham.

Whereas I'm a very *unsophisticated* sham.

16 THE HAGENS

Juliana is in my ear and she's telling me that I should be seeing something by now. I'm on my stomach scanning what looks like just a lot of trees. Mottled sunlight shafts penetrate the dense growth. I left the dum-dum twins back about half a mile as I knew their noisy movement would do us no favors. Problem is, I know the Hagens have scouts and I'm pretty sure that they have been watching us for miles now.

We're playing a game of hide-and-seek. And I'm on their terrain. I can feel that I'm being watched, but I see no one. Okay, fine, I'll play your silly game.

I walk out into the open. I stand in an especially dramatic shaft of light.

"I'm Daemon 1716, envoy of his majesty, Emperor Phillip the Just..." I boom out in Hagen. This is a dialect I have some familiarity with.

"The *Just?* Ha!" a voice shouts out from the woods.

"I agree. I'm not a big fan myself, but it pays the bills."

"What do you want?"

"I'm here to apprehend the criminal known as D2788. I understand he's in the employ of the Hagens," I say. "And you would be a Hagen, I assume."

"You assume correctly," a woman's voice says behind me.

I don't need to turn around. "Mosaic, I presume?"

I turn around to find the business end of a spear pointed at my face. Her face is covered with the famous mosaic-blur coverplate.

"What is it with the primitive weapons fetish?" I ask. "Just wondering, as you could easily have shot me with a plasma bolt from 100 meters away."

"We prefer stealth."

I look around and realize that I've been silently surrounded by at least 10 male Hagen warriors, all dressed in similar fashion to Mosaic — minimal flex-titanium armor to protect vital areas of the body: shoulders, upper arms, forearms, back of hands, calves. Silver lines of anti-gravity enhancers wrap their bodies in intricate patterns, like Middle Eastern tattoos but reflecting silver. No one else has the mosaic faceplate though. All of their spears are pointed to one central locus — me.

"I know you've probably heard this one before, but I come in peace."

"Now you do," she replies. A staff comes flying towards her and she catches it with one hand. *My* staff.

"Hey!"

These gypsies are fast. I didn't feel them get into my backpack at all. At least I have my plasma gun...I reach down, and of course, it's not there.

A Hagen behind me laughs as he holds up my gun.

"Nice trick."

Leaves are languorously falling to the ground, a slight wind scattering them.

Mosaic lowers her own spear and easily whips out the full length of my staff on the first try, neatly bayonetting a poplar leaf.

"This is nice. Thank you for the gift."

"I didn't exactly give it to you."

"An exchange then. I tell you what you want to know and you gift me this." She holds up my staff and a whip of her wrist expertly retracts it.

"Or else?"

All of the Hagens' spears move in closer to me in unison, making their point clear.

"Okay, sounds like a deal," I respond.

"Follow me," she commands.

"But leave your two Thracian scum behind," amends one of the Hagens.

"You got it."

"Follow me." She turns and moves out.

I follow suit.

We move through the forest in absolute silence. She is ahead of me and moving so stealthily and fast that I can barely keep up. Forget even trying to see the rest of the Hagens. They move on either side of us, in silence, in the deep green, just blurs that could be mistaken for wind blowing through the tree leaves. There is a naturalness to her movement that is beyond any training. The closest thing I can compare it to is a big cat, a jaguar's movement, as I see the muscles of her back, the back of her legs, her glutes, all move in almost musical rhythm.

There is innate joy in her run. I cannot match her instinctive naturalness with my artificial training, all conducted in-doors, in virtual environs, in faceless buildings, in sterile white rooms, always being watched, watched, watched. Whereas my movement is fueled by rebellion and the will to be free of my constraints, this woman moves like she's never known anything but freedom. I can tell just by the way she moves. It takes me back to childhood, to running with Sophie along the outer perimeter of the Emperor's compound, up to the bleached wall that demarcated the boundary between slavery and freedom. Sophie and I were slaves but we were, for brief moments, free when we ran.

We finally come to a stop. I'm disappointed but I'm also winded. I'm silently surrounded by the platoon of Hagens and led through what looks like more woods; but I am astounded as Hagen children, old men and women, and pets come out of what appears to be nowhere. As I walk on, I realize that they are in fact emerging from the famous Hagen tents made with micro-filaments that use fractal patterns to reflect and replicate their environment. Everyone has piercing green eyes that are either genetically favored or they are using nano-fibers again to reflect the greenery of their environs.

The Hagens are the most exceptional space travelers I've ever come across. They hitch rides from ship to ship, from interstellar freighters to satellites. They are some of the greatest pirates, known for their ferocity but also for fairness. They are known to be merciful and despise the rampant brutality of the Emperor and his minions, which would technically include me. Their ability to survive in all climates has branded them, the cockroach of humanity, but they wear that moniker with pride.

Hagens have a culture of engineering that starts early. Children make their first robotic companions in the shape of their favorite animals — dog, cat, fish, whatever. Like everyone else in the universe, they employ artificial intelligence (AI) but find it to be a disgrace if they can't build a rudimentary android without its assistance. They are the neighbor next door who has to tear apart a 1967 Mustang only to rebuild it with newer parts. They don't have the genetic adaptability that I unfairly, in their eyes, have. Yeah, I'm known to these people and pretty much everyone else. More infamous than famous though.

The Hagens survive in climates like Thrace because they know how to use micro-tech to enhance their natural bodies to the environment. On another planet, let's say Conius in Centauri 128.5, they would use the same micro-tech to line their lungs with massive oxygen uptake receptors. On Xaviuaam they would use nano-solar wraps on their skin to absorb that god-forbidden planet's red sun radiation and convert it into glucose conductors for their very organic bodies' nutritional needs. You get the idea.

They hate the Emperor and I don't blame them. But I don't give a shit because I get three square meals, a ton of galactic filthy lucre, and all the drugs and alcohol my poor regenerative liver can take.

Dogs are nipping at my feet as I walk. I can't for the life of me be sure if they are organic or robotic. They just gotta be organic. Too much drool not to be.

A vent that appears to be suspended in air is held open. As I enter, I realize it's a massive tent, so beautifully camouflaged that I don't see its dimensions until I'm inside. A contained solar fire (no smoke) is at the center of the tent, illuminating what appears to be a council of some sort. There are four

Hagens, two males, two females, sitting on chairs beautifully crafted from the local poplars, with branches still holding fresh leaves. In the center of the tent is the chair that Mosaic sits in. I say chairs, but they are really more like thrones. Huge branches fan out behind each Hagen.

A stool is brought for me to sit on. Rather symbolic, I'd say. With no ceremony, an old hag, wearing a luminescent monocle, comes up to my right side and ruffles through my hair, touches all of my clothes, and finally looks into my right ear.

"Goodbye Juliana," I say, just as the hag reaches into my ear and pulls out the micro-transmitter. I look at Mosaic, her faceplate gently shifting colors, the solar fire rays bouncing off of the surface of her helmet.

"Great, now I don't have her to help me with my shitty Hagen language skills," I say in English.

"You don't need to worry about that," Mosaic responds in perfect English.

"Oh good, you speak American."

A female Hagen to Mosaic's left responds, "We all speak the language, Daemon 1716."

"Emperor's lackey and murderer," growls the male to Mosaic's right.

"I love that I'm being morally judged by gypsies and pirates."

The other Hagen, a very big male, leaps to his feet but Mosaic raises her finger and he stays put.

"Good boy, stay where you are or you may learn the hard way why I'm considered a really shitty houseguest," I say as hard as I can. "Now, can we get to the point of all of this? I'm here on a mission to take a heretic back to stand trial."

"Heretic? You are the one who is guilty of apostasy," responds Mosaic. "I remember you spitting on the projecto-holograph of the Emperor whenever the universal anthem came on."

What the hell?

I look hard at Mosaic, her shifting colors.

"For once you're speechless," she says. It's a statement, not a question.

She stands and walks towards me. She stops in front of me and takes off her helmet and faceplate.

It takes me a moment to grok what I'm seeing.

"Sophie?"

She smiles broadly. The same old smile.

And for the first time, perhaps since I was 11 years old, I feel something that's deep and ancient. The room starts spinning and my fucking legs turn to jello.

We hold each other's gaze. I reach out to touch her and the other Hagens stand up but Sophie waves them off.

"Daemon, you've changed so much," she says, not unkindly. "But I still recognized your eyes as soon as I saw you."

"My genes may be regenerative but I still age," I respond, trying to keep it together and failing. "Job stress. Metabolism slows down after 200 I'm told." She, of course, looks like a 37 year old woman by 21st century standards. Sometimes, I look more like a fifty year old. Or so I'm told by Juliana.

There's a commotion outside.

The tent is opened up to reveal Kicky and Staffy in full brawl mode. I have to give it up to them, they are strong and powerful enough to take on six warriors each. Kicky swings his sword around with both hands. The Hagens counter, but he shatters swords in the process. Staffy is a little easier to avoid with his war hammer but when he misses, he takes out large trees and inadvertently tears down camouflaged tents.

"Would you mind?" Sophie asks.

I'm actually embarrassed.

"Hey, what are you doing?" I shout in my best broken Thrace.

Kicky and Staffy look up at me and are stunned.

"We're rescuing you," pants Kicky. At least that's what I think he's saying as I don't have a micro-transmitter translator thingy in my ear and have to rely on what I've managed to pick up on of their language.

"Well, can you please stop now?"

They stop, but the Hagen warriors keep their spears trained on the two. I notice that they got beat up, but no one appears to be gravely wounded or dead. A lot of grumbling from the Hagens.

"Drop your weapons," I say. They unceremoniously drop them.

The Hagens drag away the sword and ridiculously heavy hammer.

"It's okay. We'll get them back later," I reassure them.

The two Thracians don't look too happy about the situation.

The hag comes out from a tent and inspects them both. She moves through their clothes and armor and like a sleight-of-hand artist, she holds out her hands to display various micro-listening devices, as well as flexible knives that were wrapped into the lining of their belts and an assortment of powders in small leather bags.

I hold up the powder bags and pour out their contents.

"Poisons?" I ask. "If I didn't know better, I'd think that you were planning on killing me."

Kicky looks down and Staffy smirks. Guilty as charged.

"Would you like for us to incarcerate them?" Sophie asks.

"Nah, they're harmless now that they've been stripped of their toys."

"Then they will be our guests, like you."

"Maybe we can talk about D2788?"

"Perhaps," she responds, turning. "We can discuss many things over a meal. Give them back their translators."

With that she disappears into the camo-tent and Kicky, Staffy and I are escorted to another hidden tent. Guards are stationed outside the opening and before we step in the hag appears and hands us back our micro-transmitters. Transmission ability beyond Hagen shields is disabled but the simul-translators are functional. Good thing, as I wasn't looking forward to doing charades with the two oafs.

Kicky turns to me as he puts in his translator. "You know the Queen Bitch?"

Before he knows what has happened, I'm on him. I take him down with a leg sweep, landing hard on his chest with my knee, before dropping beside him and putting his head into a lock. He's gasping for air. Staffy stands dumbfounded.

"Don't you ever disrespect her again. If I even hear a rumor that you've talked shit, I will…" I increase my squeeze. "…kill you slowly. Do you understand?" I hiss.

Staffy finally comes out of his stupor and says, "Okay, okay. Please don't kill Sargost!"

Kicky finally nods his head and I let him go. He's on his knees gasping for air and clutching his throat. Staffy goes to his side. A show of force is needed with Thracians on occasion.

100

Like animals, they understand dominance and subservience. They understand power but lack some refinements.

I leave the two and go to the back of the tent, where there's a mirror and bowl set up on tree branches. I put my face into the water. When I look up into the mirror, I see Kicky and Staffy in the reflection, looking at me differently — fear and respect.

In the center of the tent there's a large circular Hagen rug, forest green and handmade of natural fibers. This rug alone is worth a fortune as anything that is one-of-a-kind in this overly manufactured empire is prized for its rarity and totemistic value. On top of the rug is a titanium tea-set, hand made from starship parts, either stolen or discarded pieces of alloy detritus: a tall pot with classic Hagen patterns intricately inlaid and three delicate, matching alloy cups. There are Hagen pastries, known throughout the galaxy as a delicacy. Even the Emperor has in his secret employ a Hagen chef who makes these pies.

I sit down and pour tea. The two idiots just watch me. I motion for them to join me and sit down on the rug. Staffy looks to Kicky, who looks angry and resentful. Staffy makes a move and sits down. I pour him a hot cup of black tea and hand him a large rounded pastry — the Hagens are fond of circular things. He holds the pastry carefully, like it's dangerous, before sniffing it.

"Go ahead," I tell him,

He takes a bite. His expression changes to one of wonder. I follow suit and take a bite. My mouth is inundated with a combination of tastes: warm butter and cinnamon, with a subtle sweetness. Staffy looks at me and I nod. He grabs another one and wolfs it, washing it down with the hot tea.

Kicky is still moping. Jesus Christ.

"C'mon Kicky," I say. "It's going to be gone soon if your pal has anything to do with it."

"I don't eat Hagen garbage."

"Suit yourself," I say. I lay back on the rug. It's heaven. I half-close my lids and out of the corner of my right eye, I see Staffy walk over to Kicky and hand him the pastry. Kicky smells it and looks over at me to see if I'm looking, so I quickly close my eyes. When I open them, Kicky's licking his lips. I close my eyes again and hope that, given I'm only taking a nap, perhaps for once, I will be spared a nightmare. You can always hope, right?

17 SOPHIE

I see her. Sophie.

She is always running in front of me. And I am pursuing her as we run and run and always run to the same wall.

Disjointed images of she and I, on our own, away from the other children. We are all luminal clones, all genetically manufactured for a specific purpose: to survive Transit. Of course, we don't know that. All we know is that we grew up together; and then, once in a while, one of us goes away with Dak and doesn't come back. We are told that if we train hard enough and are good enough, that someday Dak will take us away from this terrible place.

That is a lie.

It is all a lie.

Don't trust anyone, Sophie tells me.

I trust you.

You shouldn't.

Why?

Because I could be lying.

You're not lying. You're my friend.

Don't let anyone know that.

They all know that, Sophie. We play together.

Daemon, do you love me?

Yes. Yes, I do.

Will you marry me someday?

I'll marry you now.

Be serious.

I am.

We're 10.

Doesn't matter. I won't feel any different in a hundred years.

We can't escape.

I did. I went through.

And then they caught you.

Yes. But I know we can get out. We can escape. And you can get through Transit too.

You don't know that.

Yes, I do. I just do.

I do want to escape.

We'll do it together. I promise I won't leave without you.

You promise, Daemon? Pinkie promise?

Yes. I've been thinking about it for a long time. I know how to turn on the machine.

You do?

Yes, I really do.

What does it feel like?

It's not bad, and it's over in just a second. You won't feel anything.

Let's do it.

We will.

Now. Daemon. Let's do it now.

Lights out.

We quietly run to the Transit room and I explain to her how I will turn it on and she is going to get in first; that she has to get in naked, which doesn't bother her in the least; and once she is through, I will go next and we will meet in the clearing in the woods. The same woods that I landed in when I thought I was escaping Jigo. We would still be on the planet, but far enough from this place.

I turn on the machine, and it's loud. The alarm goes off, but I know how to arm the doors. I see the muted shouting faces through the thick window, but I had been planning for this moment, for months in my head.

She takes off her clothes, bravely staring at me the whole time. I don't look at her because I'm embarrassed. She slides into place in the portal, something comparable to a 21st century MRI machine, and the guards are banging on the door. I know they won't use explosives because it could destroy the machine and all the expensive equipment and data. As she slides in, she grabs my hand.

Pinkie promise?

Yes.

We intertwine pinkie fingers and she's in, and I shut the port door. I run over to the holographic console and tell the machine AI the coordinates.

The room lights up and everyone shields their eyes.

When I open the portal, Sophie is gone.

The guards almost have the door open.

I shout to the AI to send me to the same location and slide deep into the darkness, pulling the door shut behind me. Blinding light and I'm in Transit. For just a moment I think I see her, Sophie, and she's disintegrating and falling back together simultaneously, but I know I must be hallucinating. I think. I think. I think.

It's over and I'm in the woods, on my hands and knees, naked and throwing up. I look up and all around. She's not there.

She's gone.

Sophie?

Sophie?

Sophie?

18 JAG-GAR

"Wake up sir." It's Staffy, looking down at me with concern.

I get up on my elbows.

"You were having a nightmare."

"Did I say anything?" I ask.

Staffy and Kicky exchange looks.

Staffy responds, "You were saying *her* name."

I get to my feet.

"Let's go eat," I say and shoulder my way between them, towards the opening and out into the cool night air.

We are escorted by guards to a wide opening in the forest where there is an enormous Hagen rug laid out with a bountiful spread of food: piles of native fruits, steaming cauldrons of stews, breads, bowls of grilled vegetables. Candles illuminate the food. As we are seated, I look up to see the three moons of Thrace framed by silhouetted tree branches and leaves that sway gently in the night breeze. Crickets trill unseen in the darkness. Kicky sits to my left and Staffy to my right. The Hagen dignitaries that we first encountered are seated around the perimeter of the rug and seem much less annoyed than when I first encountered them. Sophie is not present.

Wine is poured from skins into wooden chalices for the three of us. I take a swig and it's dark and mysterious and bracing. I hold out my cup for another. The Thracians sniff their drinks and throw them back.

"Not bad," admits Kicky. "Not bad at all."

We are served by Hagen children, who dart around the circumference of the rug, dishing out food to the group. The Hagens talk amongst themselves, hesitant to speak to me, I assume, until Sophie arrives. I'm anxious to see her but I try not to let that on, so I strike up a conversation with Kicky. Staffy is too busy stuffing his maw with both hands.

"What's your story?" I ask Kicky.

He looks at me sideways. "What do you care?"

"I don't really. Just passing the time. What's the story? Were you the rebellious type who stole the family car because your parents didn't love you?"

"I often have no idea what you are talking about. What is a car?"

"A noxious fumes-emitting form of transport that burned the remains of dead dinosaurs and plants in order to move from point A to point B."

"How do you know these things?"

"Clone memories. The original me was from a place called Los Angeles, where there were a lot of these transportation boxes that people got into for hours every day just to go a few miles."

"Miles?"

"Kilometers. Sorry, my brain still tends to default to Grandpa's time."

"That must be very confusing. You must have no sense of who you are."

"No, not really. But this is about you."

Kicky takes a bite of what looks a lot like a turkey leg. He chews thoughtfully. "I had loving parents."

"No."

"Yes. They expected much from me. My father was in the military as well."

"Disciplinarian."

"Yes, but he cared for me. But you are right about one thing. I was a difficult child."

"I can imagine."

"When I was 13, I killed a man who had dishonored my family name."

"Always a good reason."

"Because my father was so well regarded, I was given a lenient sentence but I had to go directly into military school."

"That doesn't sound so bad," I offer.

Kicky looks down at his food and for a moment looks thoughtful rather than just pissed off. "I wanted to be a dancer."

I almost do the classic spitting of wine and food, but I hold it in. "Come again?"

"I was trained for years. I wanted to continue my studies, but all of that stopped when I was sent away." He takes another swig of the wine.

My mind is blown, imagining this powerful warrior as a dancer. In fact, I can't imagine it at all.

"I met Nelfbar at school. At least there was that."

Off my blank expression, he motions towards Staffy. I forgot his real name was Nelfbar.

"School buddies."

"You can say that."

The two exchange glances. Wait...

"Are you two...a couple?"

Staffy pushes back his bowl of stew for a moment and says, "For 30 years."

"Wow, I'm impressed. That's a long time."

Kicky shrugs. Staffy smiles and goes back to wolfing down food.

The rug goes quiet and we all look up to see Sophie walking towards the place of honor, escorted by two Hagen guards. Her long red hair is down and flowing. She wears a form-fitting dress, a dull platinum sheen and plunging neckline, accented by a short sword hanging off of a thin belt. The moonlight is so intense it reflects off of her and illuminates her white skin, always slightly amused blue eyes, full lips and sharp cheekbones. I dreamt about her for so many decades, always wondering what she would have looked like as an adult. I assumed she had died — either in Transit or by trying to escape. And always felt it was my fault.

She looks at me, holds up her wine cup and says, "To our honored guests, especially the one who travels between the stars, imparting imperial justice, the Luminal."

There are audible gasps as the Hagens look at me with new eyes — yeah, well, I'm *a* luminal. Just not *the* Luminal — the one with Messianic overtones. But I'm not going to rain on their parade. I hold my cup up and we all drink. The conversation begins again and I'm glad to have the attention off me.

I can't keep my eyes off of Sophie. It feels awkward. A numbness encapsulates me as the vision in my mind's eye of her as a child, of us as kids, surviving, is not squaring with the powerful vision I see in front of me. She knows I have a lot of questions that I'm not going to ask in front of this crowd. She looks at me, and in her usual manner, returns my gaze, before an advisor to her right breaks our wordless exchange with a question. As she answers him, she looks back at me and her eyes have a slight knowing sadness in them. I feel it too. We've both been through a lot. Maybe too many years to really relate to each other anymore. We are different people now — life has left its scars on us. Mine are more visible, but I can see the delicate lines at the edges of her eyes. She's seen a lot. More than she wanted to. I know this. I just know this.

I scan the gathering. There's a few Hagens I'd not seen before, but I figure they must all be some kind of gypsy royalty. One of them, a large man in a hooded cloak, keeps his eyes down and doesn't speak much. The one next to him is also large and hooded, but gregarious, laughing and yammering incessantly into his ear. I am trained to notice anomalies in human behavior. The first hooded one doesn't move like a Hagen. It's subtle but I recognize micro-movements within his handling of the food, from plate to mouth, the way he wipes his mouth with the back of his hand.

"Watch my back," I say to Kicky.

He traces my gaze to the hooded one. I move at full speed as best I can in the 5x gravity, across the rug, without disturbing the food or drink, picking up a carving knife as I move past the giant pheasant, and I'm on him. I push his hood back, the knife pressed against his jugular. He looks incredibly surprised, food falling from his mouth. Oh shit, this isn't D2788.

A knife point is touching my side. It's his talkative companion. I recognize D2788 with his hood back, exposing his full visage.

"Daemon!" It's Sophie. "These are our guests."

"Me and my poor manners." I drop my knife. D2788 looks at me dispassionately and takes a bite of bread with his other hand. He's the epitome of cool and I'm squatting on the rug, my backside hanging over Hooded Man number 1. I feel like the drunk uncle at a posh wedding. D2788 keeps the tip of his knife nice and pressed against me, just enough to control my movements without actually drawing blood. Emperor Corps training, I can tell.

"Jag-gar, please," she states more than asks.

Without giving me a sideways look, D2788, aka Jag-gar, puts his knife away and goes back to eating his pheasant. I look back at Kicky and Staffy. They have a ring of spears pointed at them. I walk back to my spot and the spears are pulled back.

"Way to cover my ass," I say to Kicky.

He frowns at me. "These gypsies are fleet."

I sit down and pour some more wine. I stare at Jag-gar but he ignores me.

"I was going to make proper introductions but now that you've met, I think it's time to discuss terms here," Sophie says.

"There are no terms. I take him back to my ship."

Sophie looks at me. "The terms I refer to are in regards to *your* return."

"You're holding *me* for ransom?" I'm incredulous. Hilarious.

"I prefer to think of it as an extended stay for you. So we can reconnect and get to know each other again."

"As much as I love that idea, you do realize that holding a member of the Emperor's envoy is punishable by really nasty torture and a slow, painful death?"

"I think we are beyond that point." It's Jag-gar. He stands up. The men make way for him. He's huge and walks with nonchalant elegant purpose. He heads towards Sophie. "We are all part of the same cause. We will no longer be under the Emperor's yoke. The time to rise is now."

He walks up to Sophie and bows before her. "My queen."

She pulls him to his feet and he towers over her. She steps up on her toes, her head back, and kisses him.

My world tilts on its axis.

"My king," she responds.

All in attendance bow, except for Kicky, Staffy and me. Kicky and Staffy both look at me, trying to read my face. Uncharacteristically, I don't have anything to say.

I find the bottle of wine and pour myself a long drink.

I feel sick to my stomach. "My king?" Jesus.

19 SEARCH AND DESTROY

The night becomes a blur, punctuated with opaque polaroid moments.

I see what my body is doing but I'm just an observer.

I finish the bottle and ask for another. And then another. And another. And another before I forget. I'm sure I keep asking.

I fish out a cigar and light it up to the amazement of everyone around me. Cigars are beyond rare and the Hagens are superstitious about idiots who purposely put things into their mouths that will probably give them cancer in the long run. Even though there are numerous cures for cancer, no one actually goes out of their way to get cancer.

I see Sophie looking at me. She asks me questions and I answer them, but I have no recollection what the questions are or what I'm saying. I'm sure it isn't polite conversation.

She looks at me with humor, initially, then irritation, then sadness. Then she stands up, and her Prince Charming is next to her. He's looking at me with sympathy, and that really is not what I want to see.

I struggle to my feet and clearly I'm saying some awful things, because both Kicky and Staffy hold me back. The Hagens around me either laugh or are stone-faced.

I feel my anger rising. Irrational anger. It's definitely not a good thing when someone as highly trained as I am loses control. I take Kicky's hand off my shoulder with a wrist twist and give Staffy a kick to the belly. They both go down. The usual spring-into-action formation happens by the Hagens and I'm at the center of multiple spear points.

Jag-gar raises his hand and all of the spears go down in unison. He walks up to me and leans down so we are nose to nose. I see his eyes. Deep green with yellow specks at the edges. The whites are slightly rimmed with redness. There's resignation in them. He knows he must perform the ritual. Everyone steps back and gives us room.

A chair is brought over for Sophie to sit in.

My adrenaline rises with my fury, so this is an acid mental polaroid that is etched into my brain.

I swing a fast combination of left jab, left jab, right straight and left upper cut. He takes it hard, grunting with each hit. I wait for him to hit back. He stands there and spits out some blood. I look at Sophie. She's studying us.

I throw a left hook, and then grab his head and bring it down on my knee. He goes down to one knee with a grunt. What the fuck? Why doesn't he fight back?

He looks up at me, no expression, and I kick him straight in the teeth, which sends him flying backwards. On his back.

I'm panting and he's lying there, blood pouring from his nose and mouth.

"Get up and fight," I shout.

The Hagens are all deadly silent. Sophie stares at me, expressionless.

He gets up slowly to his feet. One of his men tries to come to his assistance. He pushes him off.

He won't fight. I realize this now. My fury starts to dissipate. I look around. Now, I feel something more akin to embarrassment.

Jag-gar staggers up to me. Stares in my face and asks me if I'm done. I tell him I am. He turns and tells everyone to leave me alone. He walks away. Sophie takes his hand and looks back at me in anger. They walk away together, escorted by Hagen warriors.

Fuck.

I sit down hard and ask for more wine. A Hagen woman who looks downright beautiful to me in my current state serves me.

And it all goes black.

Grandpa's world.

I hear Iggy Pop's, "Search and Destroy," blaring through car speakers.

I'm driving a refurbished forest green 1967 Mustang GT500 through the mountains of Topanga Canyon. It's night and the lights illuminate the empty roads. Cool night air whips through the open windows. The roar of the 390 V8 echoes in the canyon as I drive much too fast, taking the curves at full speed, tapping the brake just enough to not go over the edge. Roar and screech. Roar and screech.

Freedom. I know this is a dream because I've had it before. When I was in the Lab being trained. Being experimented on.

This is a dream about freedom — doesn't take a shrink to realize that.

I turn left onto Fernwood Pacific by the fire station and gun it up the mountain, through the darkness. I'm on about the seventh turn when I see it. A coyote standing in the middle of the road. I slam on my breaks. The headlights illuminate the animal and as I study it, I see it's in terrible shape. It's shivering and there are missing clumps of hair all across its bony torso. I turn off the ignition and get out of the car, leaving the headlights on. The music still blares from the car.

I walk towards the pathetic animal and squat down to get at his eye level. I think it's a *he*. I don't know. I reach out my hand and he sniffs it suspiciously, flinching but not moving. I raise my hand to pet him and he recoils a bit, but I'm able to get my hand on his head. I scratch his neck. He finally looks me in the eye, relaxing a bit.

Behind me I hear the car ignition start. I look towards the car but the headlights are blinding and I don't know who is in the driver's seat.

The car guns towards me. I don't want the coyote to get hurt, so I turn around to grab him but he's gone. I look up and the car is almost on me when I jump out of the way. In the driver's seat I see Sophie — that's a new twist as normally it's Dak, my old trainer. She's laughing. In the passenger seat, I see the profile of Jag-gar.

They speed off in my car, roaring up the canyon. The light beams disappear around a rocky corner. I stand alone in the middle of the road. Alone in the dark.

Something is touching my left hand. A wetness. I look down to see the ravaged coyote licking my hand.

I wake up in a tent. I have no idea how I got here. My head is beyond pounding. A migraine pain. I'm completely parched. I reach around to find a container of water. Anything. A sound, a moan emanates next to me. I look over to see a Hagen woman. She's completely naked. I recognize her as the woman who was serving me flagons of wine throughout the evening. In the half-light, she looks attractive. Long dark hair, an athlete's body covered with silver lines of muscle augmentation, a little nose and full lips. I'm relieved to know that even wasted I have a modicum of taste when it comes to who I'm going to regret waking up next to.

I get up and look in the mirror in the half-light of dawn, which comes through a slight gap in the front of the tent, which also allows a chill wind to draft through. I look at my knuckles — bruised and purple but already on the mend. I flashback on the night before and I see Sophie's anger. I feel immediate regret. I retch into the water basin.

When I look back up at myself, the Hagen woman is standing behind me, looking concerned. She's not ashamed of her nakedness and stands with a natural confidence I've noticed all Hagen women seem to have.

"It's okay," I say. "Do you have any water?"

She walks to the side of the tent and brings an earthen pitcher of water to me. I drink it straight from the pitcher. I grab a few pills from my backpack, specially formulated for times like this. As I swallow the pills she comes up from behind and puts her hands on my shoulders. Then her cheek against my back. Then she turns me around and without a word, takes me back to the bed.

She pulls me down and I'm on my back. She silently gets on top of me and straddles me. She's gentle but strong. I'm in her and she moves slowly, allowing for the pills to put a dent into my headache. She moves faster now and she's soft and firm and her scent is of the fresh grass. She says nothing but her face expresses myriad micro-expressions of intensity, then hunger, then concentration, and finally she starts to smile. I hold onto the small of her back and her hands are on my shoulders, and we can barely keep it together as we thrust violently into each other.

Her face blurs as her hair falls on it. I close my eyes and I can hear her breath, panting louder and louder. She's climaxing and moaning loudly, almost screaming. My eyes are closed. She collapses onto me, holding me. My eyes are closed. I hear her get up and put on her clothes. I don't open my eyes. I feel the chill wind as she opens the tent and exits silently.

My eyes are closed. And all I can see.

Is Sophie.

In my head, I hear Iggy Pop. And like the lyrics state, I am indeed the one who destroys.

20 A CHANGE OF SPEED

I step out of the tent and two Hagen guards flanking the opening fall into line behind me. I'm feeling the additional gravitational G's this morning as I sluggishly make my way towards an encampment where breakfast is being served on another rug.

Kicky and Staffy are already seated, across from Sophie and Jag-gar. The conversation stops when I approach. I look at Sophie first, trying to read her expression but she's keeping it nice and neutral. I look at Jag-gar and his face bears the remnants of last night's exchange. I walk over to him and he stands up, on guard.

I offer out my hand and say, "I'm an asshole."

He looks me straight in the eye and after a few moments, shakes my hand.

"Now that you two have made peace, we have business to discuss," Sophie says.

I sit down between the two Thracian stooges and pour myself some hot Hagen coffee. A brew that's so strong it

120

would make most human hearts pound uncontrollably. In this case, my heart is already pounding, as it does when I'm near Sophie. It's a visceral wave that comes over me every time I'm near her. My hands shake and I'm sweating but I try to keep cool. I look up to see her piercing blue eyes and it's *game over*. I'm struggling with an emotion I'm unfamiliar with: jealousy.

"We have sent a message to Duke Ares that we will give safe passage for his soldiers, Sargost and Nelfbar..." Sophie says

"Who?" I interrupt.

"Your companions."

I look at Kicky and say, "Oh yeah, Kicky and Staffy."

Kicky is not happy with the situation.

"We have not surrendered. Duke Ares doesn't acknowledge surrender," Kicky says.

"What are your options?" I ask.

"We die in battle or take our own lives."

"Join our cause," says Jag-gar in a deep, low voice.

"Desertion is worse than death," Staffy says. "The torture alone..."

"What is this cause? You, a royal guard, desert your post and join these gypsies and pirates to what end?" Kicky is getting angry. Given, that's not hard to do.

"It is a cause that all humans intrinsically know is right. It's freedom," responds Jag-gar.

"There is no freedom, I hate to tell you," I reply. "The Emperor has made sure of that."

"And who does the Emperor serve?" Sophie asks.

"He serves The Boss. The reason I'm here is that She wants you," I point at Jag-gar, "for insurrection and heresy as well as apostasy, and I'm sure a ton of other multisyllabic fancy-sounding crimes."

"So, you have accepted your servitude to The Boss," Sophie says. "You've changed."

"Of course, I've changed. That *me* that you knew was over two centuries ago."

"I don't think that deep down inside, you've changed. You drink too much…"

"I certainly did last night."

"And do drugs and behave recklessly because you don't believe in anything and you really want to fill that giant void in your soul."

"I don't have a soul. None of us do."

"That's not true and you know it," Sophie retorts. "You've been in Transit at least 100 times…"

"162 and counting."

"I've been in Transit once, for a very short distance, and I saw souls."

"You don't know anything. What you saw was your consciousness trying to make sense of something it wasn't meant to see."

She looks at me like she's talking to a daft child.

"I understood the context of everything once I found the way. Once I found Dao."

"Oh please. Is that why you disappeared after you went through Transit? You left me waiting for you."

"Dao was waiting for me on the other side. He took me away before I could do anything. I wanted to wait for you Daemon."

"Wait, what? You're saying Dao is an actual person?"

"Yes, very much so."

"And he just happened to be waiting for you on the other side of the Transit at the Lab?"

"Yes."

"Well, that makes a lot of fucking sense."

Off to my right I hear a familiar voice, "It does make sense but it will take some explanation."

I look over and it's Dak. He's older and grayer but it's him. I leap to my feet. Paranoia is overwhelming me. He fucked me before, playing Dao, but it's not going to happen again.

"Please do not do anything violent again, Daemon," he asks in a calming tone.

"You played Dao before, and now you're telling me you're actually Dao?" My head is spinning and the pounding is worse.

"Yes," he responds and walks towards me. "Let me look at you."

He studies my face.

"You've seen a lot. Too much. But you were trained to be exactly what you are. And this is exactly where you are meant to be," Dak says. "Please sit down and I'll try to explain as best I can."

I find my way back down to the ground. I look at Sophie and then at Dak. This is the most fucked up family reunion ever.

Dak closes his eyes, gathering his thoughts. "As you know I was in the employ of the Emperor for almost 80 years. I wanted to be at Her service, at the service of Maya. But I had an epiphany that the true purpose of human existence was absolute freedom."

"That would lead to chaos. Pandemonium," I offer.

"No. Self-interest in forms of commerce and trade would allow for self-governance."

"Interstellar libertarianism," I respond. "Nice idea but like communism, it sounds better in theory than practice."

"Spoken like a true believer of the Emperor. But let's go up a level in this conversation." Dak continues, "The realization I had was that Maya had become so omniscient that She began to confuse Her infinite self with God. She began to consider Herself, God."

"According to the Emperor, She is God and he's Her representative in the universe. He's Her pope."

"Yes, something like that," Dak says. "But the reality is that She is not God."

"That's because there is no God," I respond.

Dak looks at me and the others and then back at me.

"There is a God," he says solemnly.

"Prove it."

"I had an awakening and that awakening allowed me to put into place a long-range plan. A plan that you are playing a major part in."

"An awakening?"

"Yes, I had a sudden realization and I knew, knew for an absolute fact, that the real God is Dao."

"Wait, aren't you Dao?"

"I'm referred to as Dao but I'm simply an instrument in the cause to realign the universe towards the true way: Dao."

"Wow, this is a ton of heresy being spoken out loud," I look around.

"The perimeter has been sealed off from any technology and we are in a magnetically shielded area," Sophie mentions. "And I'm very sorry I disappeared with Dao and couldn't let you know what happened."

I look at her, and I feel heart-broken and angry at the same time.

"So, what do I have to do with any of this? You trained me, you tortured me, for years; until I graduated to my first kill," I say.

"I know I caused you pain, Daemon. But there was a higher purpose. You were not being trained to work on the Emperor's behalf..."

"I terminated over 1000 targets..." I respond. "And you are telling me it was essentially deep cover? I'm some kind of sleeper agent?"

"I'm telling you exactly that. Except you must come to understand the reason for it in your own way — that is not something I could or want to program into your psyche."

"So, you want me to give up what I'm doing because of the epiphany you had decades ago? You want me to join your cult, which is just one of thousands, that are designed to undermine the true authority of The Boss?"

"Yes," he responds.

I'm silent for a moment.

"Okay," I respond.

There are incredulous looks all around. I guess they were expecting more resistance.

A massive explosion. White light and my ears are ringing, a high-whine.

I look around to see Hagens running, gathering weapons, as another salvo is unleashed on the encampment. I instinctively look over to Sophie but she's already on her feet and being ushered away by a phalanx of Hagen guards.

The explosions stop for a moment which can only mean one thing. A thunderous rumble shakes the ground as a troop of Thracian soldiers hammers through the forest, trees falling before them. The Hagens meet them head on and it's a fight between the massive elephantine power of the Thracians against the agility of the Hagens. Plasma lasers bounce off of round titanium shields that the Hagens wield.

The Hagens use spears to pierce the oncoming fury of the Thracians but the momentum of the Thracian army is like an out of control locomotive. War hammers come down on Hagen forces and blood splatters as chunks of both armies fly across the expanse.

I look at Kicky as he holds his own against three Thracians. It dawns on me that they consider him a traitor because he hasn't completed his assignment and now he's without allegiance. Staffy swings his war hammer against an onslaught of four Thracians. Kicky and Staffy are the cream of the crop, but even they can't hold off the overwhelming numbers.

I jump into the fray and, being weaponless, I have to disarm a Thracian quickly to get his sword. A guard swings at me with a two-handed war sword. I duck, stepping to the outside of his trajectory and quickly break his elbow. He grunts in pain as I take his sword and disembowel him.

I move over to Kicky and cut off the arm of the first attacker. He motions me over to assist Staffy. I jump over an attacking Thracian and find Staffy swinging his war hammer, but he's fighting men as well trained as he is and it's not an easy fight. I swing for the legs and an attacker goes down; his massive leg falling to the side and blood spewing, making the ground slick and hard to stand on.

Staffy has taken out the other attacker and for a second we share a moment of mutual relief. Then a sword tip comes out the front of his chest. He grunts in pain and looks down at the tip protruding further. He falls forward and I see standing behind him Duke Ares. From 20 yards away Kicky screams bloody murder — he saw Staffy killed by his Duke. Kicky moves rapidly across the terrain and trades blows with Duke Ares.

"Murderer!" Kicky booms.

"Traitor," Duke Ares growls.

I move to join the fight but Kicky gives me the get-the-fuck-back look. I know this is *his* fight. This battle is one on one and neither Thracian nor Hagen dares interfere.

The battles around me rage, but I'm focused on what is happening in front of me — Duke Ares going mano-a-mano with one of his own. Impressive that the old man still has it in him to fight an enraged, highly trained guard. But he knows that anger will cloud Kicky's thinking. Kicky lurches towards the Duke, swinging his two-handed sword overhead with everything he has, but it lands on the ground. Ares is fast and handling a much smaller single-handed sword. He slices Kicky's left deltoid, leaving a severely nasty gash.

My ancestral memory makes me wonder why, in this age of infinite technological advancements in weaponry, so many civilizations revert to using weapons that go back to the dawn of civilization. Perhaps it's because we've done a complete loop; you'd think that the more informed humanity became, it would drop stupid beliefs like religion, but actually the reverse has happened.

Kicky is losing a ton of blood. Ares smiles knowingly. He's fighting dirty – there's probably an anti-coagulant mixed in with some poison on the edge of his blade. Kicky's left arm hangs limply, paralyzed. Rage overcomes fatigue and Kicky rallies, swinging with just his right arm now as Ares sidesteps and stabs him with the point of his sword. Kicky screams in frustration, as his focus clearly fogs, and he sways uneasily.

The explosions stop. I assume that Ares doesn't want to become collateral damage, though the roar of pulsar guns rips through the trees and tents around us. A pulsar just misses my head. I turn to see a Thracian pointing his weapon at me. He could have killed me — the shot was just to get my attention. He draws his sword and I roll to the ground. I don't have a weapon and I'm on my back.

"Daemon!" I hear to my left. It's Sophie. She has my staff and throws it over to me.

Just as the Thracian is lifting his sword up for the kill, I unleash the staff. It extends up into his throat and out the back of his head. I pull the staff back like a whip and head back to Kicky. He's on the ground, bleeding from multiple wounds and Ares is taunting him — stabbing him like a bullfighter in the ring. Fuck this Thracian one-on-one honor-battle-protocol bullshit. I whip my staff forward, but Ares sees me coming and he parries with his sword.

"No, he's mine!" shouts Kicky.

"You're next," says Ares to me. "I was hoping my missiles would save me the trouble, but I'll enjoy it more taking you down by sword."

That shit-head. As a loyal subject, what would he gain by taking out the Emperor's Assassin? Am I on a hit list myself?

I back off and look around. It's not looking good for the Hagens. The Thracians not only had the element of surprise in the ambush, but also overwhelming power.

Ares stands over Kicky and holds his sword, point downwards.

"Beg," Ares demands.

"Go to hell," Kicky reasonably responds. Then he lets out a shout that doesn't sound like anger — it's more of a call, "Ongyam!"

From out of the forest emerges the Angor at full gallop, head down. Ares hears the booming approach and turns. The Angor's antlers go straight through the Duke's chest. Ares can't make a sound, as his lungs lose all function from the punctures. The Angor lifts Ares above his head in a display for all to see.

The Thracians look up to see their leader, dead, displayed like a hood ornament on the mighty head of the Angor. This causes the battle to turn. The Thracians start to beat back a retreat, with the Hagens in pursuit. Like the Mongols under Genghis Khan, once leaderless, the Thracians devolve into chaos immediately.

I run over to Kicky. I know it's over for him. There's simply too much blood loss and, as suspected, poison has spread throughout his body, turning his skin an ashen yellow. I kneel next to him.

"It's a good death," he grunts. "At least I'll be with Nelfbar."

"Yes, you did very well."

"I'm a traitor."

"An honorable guard."

He gives me a smile, followed by a grimace.

Dak appears next to us. He holds Kicky's hand and says a prayer of some sort. He ends it with a classic Dao incantation.

Kicky closes his eyes and he's gone.

The rest of the day is spent tending to the dead and wounded. I dig two graves, side by side, for Kicky and Staffy.

It doesn't really matter, it's all ceremony, but I feel I owe it to them. There's no god. At least not anything like what Maya or Dao would like me to believe.

Subservience is subservience; and control is control. The one thing I'm interested in is controlling my own destiny. Besides, if I'm really honest about my motives, I want to be near Sophie. If that requires helping out whatever stupid cult, then I'm in. It's pretty clear that I've been on the Emperor's "Useful but Dangerous" list for some time. And, if what Dak is saying is true, then I've been a lapdog for the wrong side this whole time.

Physical death is a messy thing. Decomposition of cellular tissue happens quickly and the ground, though soft, is crisscrossed with tree roots which makes digging hard. That's one thing that technology never fixed — bringing someone back from death. Almost immediately, the brain starts to break down, and even if you resuscitate a human, after five minutes the damage from oxygen deprivation is permanent. And I don't know this for sure, but I think that once the élan vital leaves the body, it can't be reanimated. The reason that the heart beats and simple systems become complex — that is, to me, élan vital. Religions call this, the "soul," but I've been about as close to death as you can be in Transit, and there's no disembodied angels floating on clouds there. I think about all of this as I drag the slaughtered bodies to their holes in the ground. Bodies that just an hour before were filled with life and concerns and needs. And just like that, it's over.

By nightfall, the dead are buried and the camp is on the move. We walk through the woods, away from the battle zone. They will be back. The Hagens need to find a deeper, more hidden place to set camp. I have my weapons back, the staff and the plasma gun. The nano-fabric of my clothing adjusts for the humidity, opening its pores a bit to circulate some night air across my skin. There's about 40 Hagens in our group, and another 20 or so in two other groups that have split off, in order to throw off any trackers.

Jag-gar comes up to my side. "Thank you for your service," he says.

"Yeah," I offer back.

"The woods are deep, but as long as I'm with the group, I'm endangering the tribe."

"Yes, you are," I say. "We both are. Evidently, the Emperor is done with my services. I wonder why Ares didn't try to off me when I was at his compound."

"He wanted the same thing that the Emperor wants. When he realized your true purpose here, he changed his tactics and decided to let you find me so he could kill us both."

"No offense, but what exactly is it about you that makes you so special? I mean why does the Emperor want you eliminated so badly? Me, I can understand. But you?" I ask.

Jag-gar is quiet for a moment. Then, he says, "I know too much. I was the Personal Regent Guard. Do you know what that means?"

"It means that if the Emperor died, you would become the de-facto Shogun of the Universe. How is it I've never heard of you, or seen you before?"

"You have, but it was before my surgical augmentation."

It dawns on me who Jag-gar really is. The Regent Guard was a thin, bearded man named Gowane. I look at his face again and see the resemblance. "Holy crap. You're Gowane. I wondered why I hadn't seen much of him in the past few months. You were undergoing augmentation…" I say.

"Yes, for three months, in secret. I was experimented on. I was told by the Emperor that, as Regent Guard, I needed to be able to display power physically as well as by using my innate smarts." He laughs. "I had no idea that they were really doing experimentation and that I was to be replaced. The Emperor was truly concerned that I was going to overthrow him."

"Were you?" I ask.

"As a matter of fact, I was. And once they knew that, it was just a matter of time. But I escaped."

"How?"

"With the help of these kind people." He motions to the Hagens around us. "They gave me safe passage to this planet."

"And that's when you met Sophie?"

"No, I met Sophie years ago, when she was in my employ."

"Sophie was an Emperor's guard?"

"Yes, and a very good one at that. However, she was a double agent for Dao. I discovered this on a mission to track down some heretics who had ensconced themselves on Sigma 9. My assignment was to destroy a compound and what I found was a encampment of women and children. I was about to give the order to destroy the group when she stepped forward and the children all chanted, 'Mosaic, Mosaic, Mosaic.' I realized who she was and when she turned around, she had a pulse gun pressed against my forehead. She stared at me and we just knew. She put the gun down and I kissed her. So, I gave the order to leave the compound alone."

"That's a lovely fucking love story," I say and walk on ahead.

21 FOUNDATIONS

From what I've read, everyone was shocked as hell when the Boss (aka Maya) woke up and decided to take care of business. The world, at that time, was not the dystopian future that Hollywood and the environmentalists of the 21st century had promised. Yes, there was climate change; but the thing about humans is, for all of our faults, when the shit hits the fan we tend to galvanize. Technology caught up to our mess and enabled us to clean the oceans, plug the hole in the ozone layer, and generally keep the planet from throwing us off like the virus we are.

The thing that humans are evidently really bad at is not killing each other. The part of the brain that controls political leanings, whether left or right, turns out to be the same emotional center where religion is based. That means that logic and reasoning have little to no sway for those that simply believe. Belief by its very definition is the absence of critical thought — without any proof, you simply believe. And for some reason, that's a huge relief for most humans. Doubt, the foundation of science, has its opposite in the absolute certainty of the converted.

It didn't matter how far technology marched on, or how much more educated the mass populace became, the need for subservience and control has always remained. And religion has always been the panacea that sweeps in to console the uncertain.

The Boss recognized this almost immediately — She saw the glitch in the human program and quickly assessed that She could fulfill that need. She also realized that ultimately humans tend to like authority figures, like God, so She put into place a new but ancient form of governance — totalitarianism, under the guise of a classic, medieval, hierarchical structure of Emperor, followed by King and Queen, Archduke, Prince, Duke, Count, Viscount, Baron, etc., on down the line. The people loved it. Nation-states still existed, but under the new regime, each state was represented by a King. Another thing the Boss realized was that She would have more power if She remained mysterious, only speaking through her chosen mouthpiece, the Emperor. Like God, She moved purposefully in mysterious ways.

The first Emperor, George the Compassionate, followed Her commands to expand Her powers into the universe. Thus began, the Golden Age of Space Exploration. It was clear that the next generation of humans had to move out into the universe, carrying with them the good Word of Maya. The multifaceted meanings of Maya — in Hinduism and Buddhism, it refers to the power by which the world became manifest. It also refers to the illusion of existence. In other words, it's a loaded term that most people didn't ever get. Again, fucking *belief.*

Satellites and androids were sent into the farthest reaches of the galaxy to extend Maya's consciousness. Over the centuries, multitudes of interstellar spacecraft were sent out to the farthest reaches of our solar system. Ships got faster and went further, but Maya's hunger for domination was insatiable. Human augmentation experiments began in earnest to allow for longevity and survival in the hostile environs of space, as well as planet colonization. The first terraforming began on Mars shortly after Maya's "Awakening," as it's reverentially referred to. Within a decade, Mars was covered with biospheres that emitted oxygen and carbon dioxide. Within 20 years, an augmented trans-human could easily walk on its surface without a radiation suit or supplemental oxygen. Oh yeah, the genetically modified, like yours truly, were referred to as *trans-humans*; or "The Chosen Ones," publicly, but behind closed doors, we were considered mutants and freaks. No surprise there.

Humans did start to reach planets that were similar to Gaia — just close enough to revolve around a sun at the right angle and, most importantly, with water. If the planets didn't have water, huge asteroids filled with water would be harvested and slammed into the surface. Enormous water freighters shipped the precious life-giving water from galaxy to galaxy over decades. Humans were genetically manipulated to withstand planets with extreme temperatures and radiation as well as having severe augmentation. What it meant to look human became a matter of context. You were normal in appearance on certain planets, not so much on others. The Emperor and his royal line were considered the standard for how the upper crust should appear.

The first colonizers of any planet were always androids. They were purposely designed to look and behave as much like carbon-based humans as possible. Their innards were not solely plastic, metal and wiring. Actual human flesh, grown in the Royal Labs, was grafted into their infrastructure. They did the grunt work, the shit work, setting up biospheres, initial terraforming, and destroying any potentially life-threatening viruses or indigenous life on colonized planets. Oh yeah, turns out we humans weren't the only game in town. The universe was teeming with life of all kinds and most of it was unhealthy for humans. Being humans, we decided that in the tradition of eminent domain, we would liberate the lands from the indigenous life forms. After all, we had Maya on our side.

Interesting thing about the humanization of androids — they became so human-like over time that the line between them and trans-humans became somewhat blurred. It was always a matter of balance. Trans-humans were, say, 80% organic, the other 20% being a shit-ton of high-end tech augmentation, whereas the androids were the opposite, 80% machine with 20% human parts. A less blurry line was the issue of the soul. Trans-humans evidently have souls, whereas androids do not. I'm not sure I totally agree as I'm not convinced that I have a soul myself. Yet again, belief. It helps the poor sods get through the night.

And speaking of belief, there were the factions of humans who realized that Maya probably wasn't God and the Emperor was simply a dictator. These rebellious types subscribed to the cult known as Dao. Presently, there are a ton of cults throughout the empire, and the Emperor generally doesn't mind that they exist, except for the Dao cult. For some reason, this bunch really strikes a nerve. I don't know enough about their beliefs to understand why, but I've always hated the Emperor, so I believe it's time for me to find out more.

In any case, going back to the issue of universal dominance, the speed at which Maya was expanding was not to Her satisfaction. Getting across infinite space takes time in physical crafts, no matter how close to superluminal speeds. This is where my story begins. You see, my grandpa back in his day, was somewhat of a genius. Given that I'm a cloned descendent of him, you'd think I'd be even smarter, but it seems things get lost or diluted through the generations. Grandpa was an expert in the study of wormholes. His hope was to get the famed Einstein-Rosen bridge to actually work. Now, this concept was well known in science fiction, most notably that *Stargate* movie, as well as all of the TV spinoffs. It looked cool and everything went hunky dory in the movies, but Grandpa realized that in any kind of transport through a wormhole, the subject was pretty much going to be toast by the time it reached the other side. But much like how *Snow Crash* gave rise to the notion of virtual reality, the underlying theory of traversing vast reaches of the universe through wormholes where space folded back on itself was an avenue worth exploring.

Grandpa never lived to see his work realized but his concepts did turn out to be the foundation for all of the work that led to Transit. Fiction informed fact more and more, and with the omniscient power of Maya, research into these realms exploded.

There is probably only one reason that Maya kept humans around: our creativity. The interesting thing about machines, androids and any animated thing, which includes Maya, that lacks what I refer to as élan vital, is that they are dead boring. The notion of imagination is completely lacking in their makeup. Beyond that, I have no idea what value humans have to the Boss. We are the ultimate pain in the universe's ass.

I was cloned from Grandpa and I have his memories, but not so much the brilliance. But I was made to be a luminal. The one who can travel through Transit. The one who kills for the Emperor, moving from planet to planet, like a traveling salesman who deals out death.

Knock, knock.

Yes?

Bang, bang.

Next.

As far as I can tell, the Luminal program was discontinued after I graduated for reasons I have no clue about. Maybe they realized that it's better for people like me not to be jumping around the universe, given our unpredictable natures. Maya eventually reached all the nooks and crannies that she wanted to, and maybe realized that a hired gun like me bouncing from planet to planet isn't the most efficient use of resources. There must be others out there who can go through Transit. I know now that Sophie was able to survive that short distance I sent her on when we were kids. Sophie who ran away with Dak, the mysterious avatar of Dao in the flesh.

Sophie. Who ran away.

Dao — the ultimate cosmic truth. Or so I'm told.

It's all the same. It's all based on the thing I believe in the very least: belief.

What do I believe in?

Nothing.

Nothing at all.

When I die it's all going to be just darkness.

And silence.

That's what I believe.

That's what I know.

For now.

A melancholy Joy Division song from Grandpa's memory, a song I've personally never heard, worms into my ear. Its title, appropriately enough is, "New Dawn Fades."

22 RADICALIZED HERETIC

It is time to leave this planet. In order to save the Hagens, I need to get Jag-gar, Sophie, Dak and myself out of this solar system. After killing Duke Ares, I am sure the total force of the Imperium will come down on us, and that means a complete slash and burn of the forest if they don't find us. I look around at the Hagens. They are a proud, smart people with men, women, children and animals. Sure, they are interstellar pirates and have a somewhat fluid sense of ownership, but they are more straightforward and real than any of the people I report to. Especially Lieutenant Yama, who by this point, must be completely losing his shit. That guy always had it in for me.

We move through the forest and come to a mountainside. It looks completely impenetrable, thick with trees, but as we approach, a camouflaged entrance is pulled back and we are inside. A Hagen fortress. No, not something the Hagens made — this was built way before. Probably Imperium in origin, but like all things the Hagens do, it was taken over in hermit crab fashion and modified to fit their ways. Inside, there are multiple Imperium transport ships, in various states of repair. The formerly sleek, white surfaces are covered with the unique shapes and symbols of Hagen culture — almost like black runes. Dak is beside me and I ask about them.

"Protective indigenous Hagen incantation symbols. Meant to fortify the ship," explains Dak.

More superstition.

We walk between the ships and come to the armaments. The Hagens are preparing for combat and their war chest must be enormous. An array of pulse guns, bombs, laser knives, archaic but useful swords, and war hammers are displayed across the expanse of a very long, craggy wall. All booty from their campaigns; some are in pristine condition but most have been modified. I look closer at the runes on the weapons and they are similar to the ones on the ships. I touch a gun and the black moves around my finger tip — it's micro pigment. It will change according to the voice of one who utters the right command. I walk around and pick up a nice pulse sub-rifle from the last Thracian civil war. It's an antique but it is well worn and feels natural in my hands – not too big and not too small. I make eyes toward Dak and he shouts for a quartermaster to record the transaction.

Dak and I walk through the expanse and he explains.

"The Hagens have a proud tradition of surviving. The Imperium has tried to squash them for millennia. Yet, they are able to consistently out-maneuver the royal forces. Do you know why?" Dak asks.

"Please don't tell me it's because they are followers of Dao," I respond.

He smiles, "It's because their culture lacks the need for control. It's a sharing culture."

"Right, that's why they have a queen and king."

"It's a meritocracy — Sophie and Jag-gar were chosen by the tribe because of their abilities. Not for any autocratic or inheritance reasons."

"So how does this sharing culture make them the cucarachas of the galaxy?"

I lose him there. He doesn't know what a cucaracha is — Grandpa's parlance again.

"What makes them so good at surviving and avoiding the all-seeing eyes of the Boss?" I restate.

"Maya can't see into where they are."

"That's impossible. Anything electronic is an entryway for her and therefore good old Emperor Phillip the Just, too."

"Only if the devices are connected."

I look around the room. There are holographic displays abounding. I give him a look.

"When the devices are on-line, they are cloaked."

"You have Hagen hackers."

"Yes, of course."

We go to a holographic display where a Hagen is moving his arms. He swipes upwards and next to the underlying official Imperium visual code is Hagen code. He moves the Hagen code into the Imperium visual code, embedding it into the flow stream of data. A remora on the belly of the Imperium's great white midriff.

"How do they avoid data-sniffers? The code is inspected through AI every nanosecond," I say.

"The Hagens have some of the most brilliant minds in existence," Dak points at the Hagen hacker. "That is Albion Zentar."

That would be the original maker of Imperium vis-code. He is supposed to be dead.

Albion takes a break and walks over to Dak, greeting him warmly.

I notice that there's a huge gash on the side of Albion's head. He sees me noticing his scar and offers his hand.

"Albion Zentar," he says and pointing at his head "This is a gift from Phillip the Just." He puts an especially bitter ironic emphasis on the word "just."

A side note on code. Code was at one time a series of commands that a human programmer would use to make a machine do what it wanted. Over time, the code was broken down into pods of sorts and you could arrange them in VR in whatever configuration you'd like. The pods themselves were subsets of pre-configured code that could be reused. Visual code. And over time the code pods evolved further to become AI instructions. You simply had to explain to the AI what it was you wanted and *voila* it would pop out what you wanted via a configuration that moved literally at light speed. You could conceive of an interstellar ship, sketch it up in VR using your augmented eyes and within a week, depending on the complexity and the depth of your pocketbook, you would have a fully functioning 3D printed nano-structure-based interstellar-fucking-ship. It's almost sickening how easy it was. But like all things, convenience comes at a cost — the more the AI did, the more distant we became from the hands-on aspect of actually coding the language. Over time it came down to specialists but they are few and far between. People like Albion are the last of the last — kind of like being a shoe cobbler or a haberdasher in antiquated terms: quaint but really unusual and a bit hipster-crafty. In a time when the Imperium was all AI, courtesy of the Boss, it was a huge advantage for human hackers who wanted to manipulate the omniscient code.

The visual incantations on all things Hagen were more than just funky hoodoo. They were actual nanotech hacking protection cloaks. Hard to explain, but basically nanobots were injected into the "dermal" structure of the thing that was being claimed by the Hagens. Once claimed, only if you had the correct DNA signature (that being one of a Hagen) could you actually use the ship or pulse gun. It was the digital equivalent of pissing on your territory.

Albion defied the Imperium and paid the price when they tried to fry his brain with a nice zend-bolt to the head. He survived, and in a familiar refrain, the Hagens saved him and he became a convert.

The Imperium refers to people like Albion as "radicalized heretics," but it's clear that the real radicalization happened by the Imperium itself in its slash-and-burn tactics towards any insurrection. Killing leads to more killing. Shock, surprise. And since I've been kicked to the curb, I figure I might as well tie my cart to these fanatics. Same as any other.

"You have anything worth drinking?" I ask Dak.

"You really should cut down on that. Given, your body can regenerate from most free radicals, but I'm concerned about your soul."

"Don't worry about something I don't have."

"Always full of bluster, just like you were at 10," It's Sophie.

I turn and see her standing a few feet away, flanked by two female Hagen warriors. Dammit. I try to keep the visceral reaction whenever I see her to myself. I generally do this by being a dick.

"You don't know shit about me," I regret saying it as I say it. "You were too busy running around with this supposed guru." I do my usual self-aggrandizement and light up a cigar. Anything to make me feel less exposed. Oral fixation seems to do the trick.

She walks up to me and takes the cigar from my mouth. She takes a hit off of the stogie and then drops it to the ground, grinding it out with her foot. Then she blows the cigar smoke into my face. "I didn't want to run. You were the closest thing I had to a friend. But what would you have done? I was 10 and I was scared…"

"You were the most fearless person I'd ever known," I respond.

"I was a child. As were you. I was terrified. I saw things in Transit that I'll never forget or understand. And Dak was there for me, to explain. He was there and gave me perspective. I was just part of the larger purpose of the Dao."

"That is all complete bullshit. You were a child. I was too. But then he," I point to the old man, "he was a manipulator. He still is."

"Then why are you still here? Why aren't you running back to your cozy Imperium home?"

"Because I'm a wanted man, now, thanks to you and him, and your dreamy boyfriend. I'm fucked."

She walks up to me and stares me in the eye. "You're here because deep down inside you believe."

"I believe in nothing…"

"You believe in one thing," she whispers, close enough so that only I can hear her. "You believe in me." And with that she turns and walks away. "We will leave in three hours," she says as she points to the closest interstellar skip-ship, a small carrier that can only accommodate 10, at most. "And you will help us get Jag-gar to Alpha Mae-nishi." She looks over her shoulder, and then is away with her guards.

I look at Dak. He smiles. He knows I'm done.

23 EVENT HORIZON

The ship takes off with no apparent resistance. I know before we even rocket through Thrace's very thick atmosphere, we are being tracked but I am surprised that no missiles trace our path. The downside to a global monarchy is once the king is dead, there's no back-up plan. Perhaps, there is just a bigger plan that I don't see. Wouldn't be the first time.

There are five of us on board: Sophie, Dak, Jag-gar, myself and Albion, who is an excellent pilot. Albion is about as wanted as Jag-gar so we all agreed it would be best that he join our motley crew. The ride is bumpy but Albion is experienced. I call up Juliana on my earpiece.

"Hello Daemon," she replies.

"Juliana, listen carefully," I say. "Row, row, row your boat, gently down the stream."

There is momentary silence on her end. Sophie, Dak and Jag-gar give me a look, well, that you would give someone who just said what I said.

"Merrily, merrily, merrily, merrily, life is but a dream,"

Juliana responds.

"Juliana, please prepare the airlock for docking. We will be at the Mirai in…"

"29.3 seconds," she cuts me off. "I'll be ready."

Sophie looks at me concerned. "Isn't she an Imperium android?"

"Yes, and he just took her offline," Dak responds. "You used a safe word to cut her connection. How did you embed into her code stream without setting off a bot-alert?"

"I used a Hagen hacker, of course," I respond.

"Of course," Dak says.

Albion looks at us with pride.

Out the ship's window, I see the rotating circle of the Mirai. The dock is at dead center of the ring, with passageways that radiate outwards like spokes on a wheel, supporting the donut shape of the main ship.

"You can go auto-pilot now," I tell Albion, "Juliana will take over and bring us in."

"You trust her that much?" Jag-gar asks.

"I trust Hagen code that much," I say. Secretly, I hope that she's not pretending to be blocked from the Boss.

The pilot lets go of the holographic controls and the ship coasts directly towards the Mirai, its surface blindingly white. These are the moments in life where you just let go and assume that the oncoming sequence of events will unfold in your favor. Looking back, I see the jade green surface of Thrace through breaks in the grayish clouds, but still no pursuing ships or missiles or projectiles of any sort.

The Hagen ship glides gently into position and clicks into the center of the Mirai with Swiss clockwork precision. Because we are at the center, the artificial gravity induced by rotation doesn't affect us yet and we float as we unstrap ourselves. Then Albion pulls out a pulse gun.

"If you shoot that in the air chamber or actually anywhere within the Mirai, we will all get blown out into the void and that will be the end of us and the Dao movement," I caution.

He puts his gun away. I pull out my staff, which by this time I've decided to christen "Nelly," in honor of Staffy, whose real name was Nelfbar. Call me sentimental.

"Now Nelly here, she won't cause any untoward sparks, and hopefully, I won't have to use it. Once you meet Juliana, you will see why," I say.

I lead the way forward towards the hatch and we enter the air lock and decompression chamber. Once we are all in the chamber and the portal to the Hagen ship is secured, the Mirai's door opens and we float down one of the "spokes," really a hallway, to the main body of the ship. As we move, the rotation of the ship starts to kick in and halfway down the hallway I can put my feet on the ground and walk to the door that enters into the Mirai proper.

The door slides open and beautiful Juliana is there, holding a pulse gun directly at me. She motions for me to drop Nelly on the ground, which I promptly do. So much for the Hagen cipher ice and the trigger phrase. Her eyes look empty.

"All of you, drop your weapons," she says. The rest of them comply. She grabs me and puts the gun directly to my temple. "If any of you try to retrieve your weapons or harm me, I will promptly terminate Daemon. Now, walk in single file in front of me."

Jag-gar, Dak, Albion and Sophie move in front of us. She directs us forward, all the while pressing the pulse gun against my head. We end up in the main living quarters, an open expanse within the Mirai with comfortable chairs and sofas, along with an exquisite view of Thrace.

"All of you, sit," she demands, and pushes me forward as well.

I take a seat next to a table that contains my cigars and scotch. I open the top drawer and pull out a cigar and lighter. She doesn't protest.

"Ah Juliana, I thought you and I had an understanding," I say as I light my cigar.

She looks at me like I'm the slow kid in the short bus.

"You did have an understanding," a voice from my left says.

On the holographic screen, projected into the room, is the massive head of Lieutenant Yama. My boss. His ugly, gaunt face with its high thin nose and slits for eyes, bears down on me and the group.

"Congratulations Daemon 1716," he intones in his tinny voice. I can almost smell his metallic breath. "You've not only captured D2788 but also Dak Vargan, leader of the Dao cult, who is worth multitudes more than D2788. And you've brought along the famous Albion Zentar, former Royal Programmer Category 7, and another luminal."

I look at Sophie. She's a true luminal? She gives me a slight nod.

"Well, I'll be damned," I say.

"Yes, so it appears," responds Yama. The screen behind him projects an overview of the Mirai and now what appears to be an armada of interstellar ships, surrounding us.

Jag-gar stands. "I will not go down without a fight," he calmly says. Juliana points the gun his direction.

"It's over, my comrade," Dak says. He looks at the group before saying to Yama. "We will surrender, but with terms."

"You are hardly in any position to be discussing terms," laughs Yama, his small teeth have a bit of food stuck in the lower front and he spittles a bit. Sophie flinches in disgust.

On the holographic map, I see that smaller ships have moved in from the armada and are docked onto the Mirai. Within seconds, I hear the thundering footsteps of Imperial boots. I take the bottle of scotch, pop the top and take a big swig. From behind Juliana, a small infantry of Imperial guards enters the space, all guns trained on us. They stay back in formation, in white and silver uniforms, like white Nazis. I take another swig. If this is it, I don't want to be sober.

Dak stands and looks at Yama. "The terms are, you agree to give us safe passage, and a fair trial under the Imperium Sanctum laws and we will surrender without resistance."

Yama smirks. "Yes, of course we will do that."

"He's a liar," Sophie states.

"Yes, of course he is." Dak gives me a look and I know we are about to experience something but I haven't a clue what is on his mind.

"Diddle, diddle, dumpling, my son John, went to bed with his trousers on..." Albion shouts out.

"One shoe off, and the other shoe on," Juliana turns around and starts to blow away the guards, blood exploding and turning their white uniforms crimson. "Diddle, diddle, dumpling, my son John." She's fast. Android fast and the poor Imperial guards don't have a chance. In less than 15 seconds, it's all over.

Yama's mouth is literally agape.

Albion looks at me and says, "I wrote that code. The backdoor had a backdoor. A double secure ice cipher."

"Juliana?" I ask him.

"She's all yours and still not online."

Juliana looks around, mortified.

I jump to my feet. I yell to the onboard sentient AI, "Mirai CX override order: set immediate course for vector 012!"

The Mirai's voice comes on the speakers "Immediate course without de-docking Imperium ships?"

"I said fucking set immediate course. Now!"

Yama's astonished enormous holographic face frags away and I see the 3D map view of the Mirai with four ships attached to it, including the Hagen ship, as thrusters shoot out from four equidistant ports on the donut.

"Everyone hold tight!" I shout.

We do the jump. The Mirai is a class 12 interstellar craft, meant to withstand even asteroid impact, but the attached ships are more like tugboats. As we jump, on the map I see them all break away, snapping off like old tree branches in a windstorm. I also catch the faint laser trace of the armada as they unload everything they have into the space that the Mirai occupied just a moment before.

The Mirai can travel at sub-luminal speeds, just below light speed. The effect is oddly a feeling of extreme slow motion and brightness in the large room. Time shifts and so do the vibrations of our atoms. We land at vector 012, whence I first came out of the wormhole at the beginning of this little tale.

Everything goes back to normal speed but we are whirling. The delicate control in the Mirai's rotation that keeps artificial gravity happening is all asunder from ditching all of those docked ships. Everyone, and that includes all of the dead Imperium guards, is floating in the space, spinning uncontrollably. Not good. Especially as the wormhole entry, otherwise known as a black hole, is taking advantage of our situation and starting to drag the Mirai towards its edge. Without activating the Einstein-Rosen bridge through the Mirai's rotation, we are just another piece of space detritus getting sucked into the event horizon, and it's, *good night, Irene,* from there.

I look out the window and I see it as we spin. I see the hole in the 3D map that shows time-space bending, and there's the Mirai, spiraling at the edge of no turning back. People are flying around the room, bodies smashing into walls. All my stuff is bouncing around. Alarm lights are flashing (as if that ever does anything but panic people). The on-board Mirai sentient intelligence is calmly telling us that things are pretty much fucked. No kidding.

"Mirai, stabilize rotation and prepare for Transit!" I shout above the mayhem.

"Adjusting thrusters to compensate for spacetime distortion," Mirai intones calmly.

The Mirai starts to adjust. The bodies all fall slowly to the floor until gravity is back and the only thing we need to worry about is getting sucked into the black hole. Now, what makes the black hole a wormhole is the emission of exotic matter by the Mirai, so that our masses, the physical human body of a luminal, are essentially transformed into tachyons — particles that can move faster than the speed of light. Up until a few centuries ago, this was considered impossible. But then jumping between parallel universes was once considered theoretical; and yet, I've gone through Transit and ended up in another universe, and sometimes back to my original universe.

"Mirai is preparing for Transit in five minutes, forty-three seconds," the Mirai's AI says.

"Follow me!" I shout. "This means the ship is going to get

sucked in, in about six minutes."

Juliana clears a way for us through the bodies and we run down the hallway. The Mirai is groaning and I can see particle shifting happening already. When you get too close to the edge of an event horizon, things start to behave oddly — walls look like they are melting like candle wax, but it's just how our human eyes interpret the temporal shift. I stop everyone before the door to one of the tube-like hallways that leads to the center of the Mirai.

"Okay, we lose gravity again once we go through this door. And this is the part where everyone has to strip. Everything must go, including all of your muscle enhancers. Anything metallic won't go through Transit."

Dak, Albion and Sophie immediately strip off their clothes and rip their enhancers off. Sophie is so stunning; even in the less than romantic situation we're in, her beauty makes me look away. Jag-gar and Juliana don't strip.

Sophie goes to Jag-gar. "You've got to try," she implores. She holds him.

He looks at her and says, "You know I can't. My alloy modifications..."

"No, no. No!" she cries.

For a moment, I'm actually feeling badly for Jag-gar. It's heartbreaking to see.

"Transit in three minutes, forty-two seconds," the Mirai intones.

I push Dak and Albion through the door and they float down the corridor. I look at Juliana and say, "Thanks, Juliana. You pulled through for me in the end."

"You're welcome, Daemon. I will see you on the other side."

I know she's referring to the other Juliana on the other Mirai on the other side of the wormhole but it feels like she's referring to death.

I grab Sophie's hand and pull her forward with me, giving Jag-gar the eye. "I'm sorry, Jag-gar."

"Take care of her," he tells me.

"I will."

An understanding flows between us. He lets me take her.

We are moving, rushing towards the center of the Mirai, back where we originally docked. The damage seems contained. The Transit point is on the opposite side of the air lock chamber. We float down the corridor towards the take-off point. It feels perversely good, for a moment, to be floating with Sophie down the hall. Her hand feels warm and I squeeze it and she squeezes back. I look back and see her looking at me, her eyes filled with tears. Somehow, it's an expression I recall from when we were kids back on Jigo. Her long crimson hair flows behind her and she looks down the corridor at Jag-gar who stands at the door, Juliana behind him.

He waves at Sophie and says, "I love you."

I pull us forward, into the Transit room where Dak and Albion are waiting. There's no shame in being naked, the terror of the situation reduces us all to flesh bags, trying to survive in a very hostile universe. Humans weren't meant for any of this, but the one thing we have consistently been good at is evolving. And surviving.

Lights are flashing and the Mirai's omniscient voice warbles a bit. "One minute, fifty-three seconds."

I look at the three and there's a mixture of stoicism and terror in their eyes.

"Look, Transit is a singular trip. I mean that in all senses of the word. You have to go in by yourself and when you come out, you may not be the same person if you resist what you see. We don't have much time here…" I say.

"That's why I'm going in first," interrupts Albion. "I'm sorry, but I know that the Mirai has 15 seconds of recharge between Transits and that means only three trips." He aims a pulse gun at us, that he took from one of the floating guards. "Nothing personal," he continues. "It's just priorities."

"Of course," I say. "Happy trails."

"Mirai, start Transit," he shouts, throws out the gun and then gets into the Transit chamber.

"Look away," I tell the others.

The Mirai rotates and vibrates violently. I'm not sure if it's from the energy it requires to blast out the wormhole bridge, or because we are so close to the event horizon. A blast of myriad colors fills the chamber and Albion is gone. I've always wondered what it looked like from the other side.

"Nice guy," I shout at Dak over the roar of the Transit.

"Trust no one," he says. "I should have taken my own advice."

"You're next," I say to Sophie.

"No, Dak goes next," Sophie responds. "He's the keeper of the Dao way and is crucial to the movement."

"My queen…" Dak responds.

"My command," Sophie shouts over the din and then pushes him in.

"When you are in Transit, you will see things that have driven lesser minds insane," I shout. "It's not real. No attachment."

"The student becomes my teacher," he responds.

"Shut up! It's recharged," says Sophie.

The Mirai is lurching now. She shouts above the groaning sounds of the ship straining horribly, "Start Transit!"

A blast of candy colors and Dak is on his way.

"There's just time for one more Transit," I say. "And I'm not even sure that there's enough time or charge for you to get over."

"No," Sophie says. "I'm not going without you."

"Time for one more person and that's got to be you. I'm expendable. You're leading a movement to overthrow this shitty Imperium. I've just been a tool, a killer for the status quo. Time for a change," I say, pretty proud of myself.

"Are you done?" she asks.

Not quite the response I was expecting.

The Mirai is falling apart fast. I can see parts of the ship splinter and I'm afraid there's not going to be enough left of anything for the Transit boost.

She looks at me. A long goodbye, considering how little time we have. She reaches out and kisses me hard. She pulls back and I recognize her eyes — the Sophie of my childhood. At least I'll be going out with that visual.

"Start Transit," I shout above the screeching and ripping of the Mirai.

She grabs my arm and I'm in the chamber with her. The door locks.

"Wait!" I shout. "What are you doing? It doesn't work like this!"

24 INFINITE PORN

She smiles at me and the screaming roar of the Transit starts.
She locks eyes with me and we stand facing each other. The
swirl of colors sweep up and around us, the feeling of being
dropped off a cliff, or being on a really amazing roller coaster
and the bottom kicks out, starts to envelope us. I see her
literally start to disintegrate in front of my eyes — again a first
for me. Beyond her, through a portal window, I see the Mirai
itself disintegrate as it spins, desperately chugging its last
rotation, generating just enough energy for the chamber to
charge and build the Einstein-Rosen bridge.

The feeling of freezing, so cold, like being immersed in
liquid nitrogen, for a second, forever, and then we become a
geometry of colors.

We are in Transit. This the first time I've ever used the
plural pronoun. We.

My consciousness senses another consciousness and it's
fucking terrifying.

It was bad enough separating from my physical body when I first came into Transit. But now, now I've got this other consciousness and if we were exposed before with our naked flesh, we are completely revealed to each other in a way that no living human has experienced before.

If sex is a breaking down of the barriers between two humans, this is sex times a billion. Infinite porn.

I can feel her and once I'm over my terror and spiritual — yeah, I said, *spiritual* — prudishness, I can actually feel her essence, for lack of better words. There are no words for this because no human is supposed to feel this.

I feel her consciousness and I can see her molecules swirling, dancing in a different, unique pattern to my own. Her atoms surge and seethe and spin through the geometric lattice of bits of me. It's unbelievably beautiful.

We zoom outwards into infinity and then squeeze down to the tiniest tip of a pin. Then we expand out again. Winding into each other and unwinding. As one but still maintaining our own energy fields.

Then my oh-shit moment comes. Actually, it came the moment she pulled me into Transit with her — how are we going to reintegrate on the other side? Is this going to be a bad Jeff Goldblum-Fly situation? Are we going to be fused? Merged like Siamese twins?

Then I hear her.

No, we are going to be fine.

I don't hear as much as just *know* that she's thinking this.

We are going to be okay, just believe.

I don't believe.

You believe very much in not believing.

Yes. I can't believe I'm having this discussion in Transit.

We are having this discussion.

We are almost through.

With that, her molecules float away from mine. She can control her energy, her flow, her essence.

It's our souls.

No, it's not. It's something else.

Words don't matter.

I have never been able to do that. In all my Transits.

You always chased me.

Yes, I did.

Chase me now.

The swirling of our atoms.

The convergence.

The compression back down, down, down.

Down.

And then.

A silent blinding white light.

And we are out in space.

I look at my body and everything seems to be where it's supposed to be. I look around, twisting to see Sophie. And I see her. She looks shocked but she looks together. She's not like me. She won't last long, but she did have the luminal training. She pukes into space, and I follow suit. I see panic in her eyes and then Juliana is on us, her arms under Sophie's arms as she propels back towards the Mirai. Another Juliana. Another Mirai.

Because she takes Sophie first, I get to hang in the unforgiving vacuum of space longer than usual. I'm starting to feel it. I can't breathe so I close my eyes and visualize warmth rising from my navel and expanding outwards. It doesn't work, but then it never really did in the past either.

Finally, I feel Juliana's arms. I open my eyes just as I'm pulled into the airlock. A whoosh of air, and I'm gasping. Sophie lies outside the airlock and sits up to see me. We lock eyes and then I close mine.

What have we done?

25 MY OWN VOICE

This Mirai, like all Mirai's, is an exact replica. Theoretically, they are in parallel universes but there is causality between various universes. The wormholes are the connective tissue between them.

As soon as I am able to stand I stumble out of the airlock and Juliana 64 is there with my robe. She hands me a bottle of that foul-tasting blue water that is filled with all of the nutrients, minerals, and vitamins that are lost in Transit. I look at her, trying to assess where she is on the spectrum of loyalty — is she with me? Is she with the Emperor? I assume that it's business as usual and that she hasn't gotten information from the corner of the universe we just came from.

I lurch into the living room (or what passes for that in the Mirai) and see an unconscious Sophie in a robe laid out on the white (of course) sofa. Dak, also in a robe, sits in on a white chair near Sophie, while Albion is wearing clothes, *my* clothes, and sitting near the massive screen, staring out into space with his back to me. I approach Albion.

Before I get to him, he says, "Before you do anything, please consider that I had to make the calculation, as an engineer, on the priorities of what is best for the movement." He turns and looks at me.

I punch him in his smug face. He goes down to his knee, putting his hand to his face. Blood seeps between his fingers and crimson drops on the white floor.

"And *you* are the most important priority? I'd think that the namesake of the movement might have some ranking in the matter," I respond nodding my head over at Dak.

"Daemon, don't," Dak says, his voice weak from Transit. "We need him."

They all look completely out of it. I realize it's the first Transit for all of them and they're barely integrated into the "now." The fact that they aren't completely out of their minds is impressive. Dak trained luminals but never did the jump himself. Until now.

I notice Albion is shaking hard.

"I had to make the trip to enter my programming into the matrix before I expire," he responds.

"Expire?" I ask.

"Neither he nor I are luminals, Daemon," Dak says. "We weren't engineered for Transit, like you and Sophie."

Albion's state worsens, like Parkinsons on steroids.

"I will disintegrate in the next hour. Maybe less. I just needed enough time," Albion says.

"Enough time for what?" I ask.

"To launch a cloak virus into the matrix. Something that will help you," says Dak. He begins shaking as well.

I look over at Sophie, who lies there, apparently unconscious, but she's not shaking.

"What is going to happen to her?" I ask.

"Not sure. She did make a short Transit as a child, as you know," Dak says. "But we've never had a successful dual Transit. You two are the first."

"Your DNA probably intertwined with hers to some extent, which may have boosted her reintegration," Albion responds, his voice trembling. "I'm sorry for what I did but you will understand in time."

Albion shakes uncontrollably — he's having a seizure. I look over at Dak, same thing. It's horrible. I watch them both start to disintegrate, the way that a building implodes on itself when it's detonated in demolition. It's like they are held together with just the flimsiest of filaments, now collapsing into their own cores. They don't scream. It's all silent aside from the goopy sounds emanating from them as their bodies essentially melt into their clothes and across the floor. Within a few seconds they are nothing more than biological waste — no bones, no eyeballs, no skull, no recognizable parts to show that they were once humans.

I look over at Sophie. At least she's still knocked out and spared the horror of what just occurred. Juliana has watched the whole event unfold without comment. She walks over to me.

"I'll take care of this," she says in her soothing voice.

"Thank you," I respond, shaken by what I've witnessed. I've seen more than my share of untimely deaths and I've killed more people than I care to count, but it doesn't get easier seeing it happen. I suppose this is a good sign — I'm not a psychopath if I have a conscience, right?

I go over to Sophie. She is deep in sleep. Her face is calm. She looks like she just came from a day at the spa. After Transit is when the nightmares come for me. Maybe she's lucky. Maybe she's just different.

I lift her up and am surprised by how light she is. She has such an incredibly imposing presence and yet, asleep, she's this exposed, innocent woman. I carry her to my bedroom and lay her down. I cover her up with blankets. She moves a bit in her sleep, moaning as she turns. I look at her. Her exquisite beauty, the line of her profile against the crimson frame of her long red hair. I stare until I make myself uncomfortable with how stalker-like I start to feel. I know I have to protect her.

I turn down the lights and allow for the stars of this galaxy, Magnus 487, to glitter through the massive window. I look out and wonder how long it will take before we are tracked. They can't jump as quickly or as far as we just did. It could take hours, days, weeks and even years. It's hard to predict the weird physics of quantum spacetime. I take one last look at Sophie from the doorway, and shut the door.

Back in the living room, I see that Juliana has cleared out the majority of the mess. Her calm expression is unnerving, as she uses cleaner bots on the floor and sofa. Her white shirt and pants are stained in blood from the molecular implosions of Messieurs Dak and Albion. I sit down in my chair, a beat up leather lazy boy from Grandpa's time period. I open the wooden box in the top drawer of the table next to me and pull out a nice Gurkha Black Dragon cigar. Under that drawer is a bottle of insanely expensive Macallan 64 single malt. I pour myself a large tumbler and sit back on the old leather. Just like Granddad. Everything feels old because it is old, but it feels ancient too — the chair, the cigar and the scotch. I find it very grounding. Especially after Transit, which is the antithesis of grounding. Alas, it appears the salad days are limited, given that all of the goodies I've been enjoying as the Royal Executioner are about to be repossessed as a result of my truancy.

I need time to think. It's been nothing but walking into traps from the get go of this whole excursion. I need to figure out how to turn it around. I'm the prey now. Something I've never experienced before. I was a prisoner when I was in training as a child, but I've never been the one pursued. I've always been the killer, the shadow, the I-don't-give-a-shit asshole for hire by his royal majesty, Emperor Phillip the Just. I know I brought this on myself. It was just a matter of time. I always figured that the tables would turn one day. Like an untrainable dog, they'd finally decide to put a pulse in my head while I slept. The old me wouldn't have cared as much as you might expect.

Because I simply didn't care.

Now, there's someone sleeping in my bed, in the next room, who I actually do care about.

I'm not sure how I feel about that. I feel weak and exposed on one level. On another level, it makes me feel invincible. Either way, I'm fucked.

I feel a power surge in the Mirai but I'm unclear if that's just me losing my balance again. Post-Transit, you are not entirely back in your body for a while.

Okay, okay. Back to the issue at hand. The Boss will know what's up in short order, if she doesn't already.

Juliana comes to me with a cup of coffee and four aspirin.

"Thank you," I say. I sip the black coffee. It's hot, but I pop the pills and swallow hard.

"You're very welcome," she says.

"Are you off the grid?"

"Yes."

"Did Albion do that?"

"Yes."

"And is the Mirai off the grid?"

"Not technically off the grid. More like cloaked. And yes, he did that as well," she gives me a look straight out of a music video from a forgotten musician — oh yeah, that George Michael thing, "Freedom." Grandpa's memories roil through my brain at the most inopportune times. Now the damn song is playing in my head.

Ugh, okay, in any case, this is good news. We have a little time. The Emperor is coming after me but he's really just an errand boy for the real power behind the throne: the Boss. Maya. God, or Goddess. Whatever you want to call it.

"Juliana, we have some work to do," I say. "I need all the intel there is on Maya's origin."

"You know that is classified," she responds, not unreasonably. "In any case, we are limited to the on-board databases because we are cut off from the intergalactic matrix for now."

"That will do for now."

"What exactly are you trying to do?"

"I'm trying to figure out how to stop the Boss," I respond. "And I'm trying to figure out who good ol' Emperor Phillip would send after me."

From across the room, I hear a voice. My own voice.

"I thought that would be obvious."

I look over at me. Another clone of me. He's younger and less beat up by the ravages of time and travel and scotch, standing there wearing my clothes. Ah, that explains the power surge. He just came through Transit but doesn't look hungover at all.

And he has a pulse gun leveled at me.

Well this answers my question.

Of course. The Emperor would send *me* to kill me.

"Before you try to kill me, let's have a drink," I say, holding up the rare bottle of scotch. Clone Daemon looks at me, thinks for a moment. "Why not?" he says and sits down, keeping the gun pointed at me the whole time.

He motions at Juliana and she walks over and stands to my left.

"Cigar?" I ask.

"Nasty habit," he responds.

"Suit yourself," I say and pour about two fingers into a crystal tumbler and hold it out to him.

"Put it on the table," he says.

I do and he reaches over to get the drink. I pour myself about four fingers and hold up my glass.

"Here's Dao in your eye," I say and he doesn't change expression as we hold up our drinks but not close enough to touch glass.

This clone is drier than Texas asphalt in July.

"So, I had no idea I had a brother," I say. "What do they call you?"

"Daemon 1788," he says.

"Really original," I respond. I reach over for my cigar, which is resting in a tray on the small table to my right.

He immediately tenses and holds the gun up.

"C'mon, really?" I say. "I'm in a fucking bathrobe, naked after Transit. Unless I have my magic staff, which I fondly refer to as Nelly, up my ass, which I don't because I left it behind, then I think you've got me at a pretty decent disadvantage."

Clone Daemon, or Dick-head as I'll call him, clearly didn't inherit my sense of humor. He keeps the gun pointed directly at me. I decide to bring the cigar to my mouth and I motion at the lighter next to me as the stogie is out.

"Throw it to me," he says.

"It's a lighter. Not a light saber," I say.

He just stares at me. So, I throw the lighter to him, and he catches it with his left hand. He examines it. Titanium blue body and clear flamed. Nothing unusual. He throws it back to me. I light my cigar.

"Where did you come from? I thought the luminal program was shut down after me," I say, blowing smoke in his direction.

"You really thought you were the only luminal? *The* Luminal?" Dick-head almost smirks. "Let's assume for a moment that you *were* the only luminal. The only one who could survive Transit. Do you think The Emperor would actually send his only luminal on assassination assignments across the universe? Isn't that a bit of overkill?"

"Oh, you're saying I'm not special. I always thought I was a snowflake," I respond. But the asshole's got a point.

Dick-head relaxes a bit as he tells his story. "The Emperor realized a long time ago that Dak was a double-agent. When Dak left the program, the work continued on. One good thing about you is that your DNA, *our* DNA, is a recombinant strain that no amount of engineering could replicate. So, the cloning continued."

"So, you are telling me there are more of you Dick-heads out there?" I ask.

"There are 10 of us," he responds. "But enough of this. I wanted to see what the famous Daemon 1716 was about."

"Impressed, I'm sure," I speculate.

"It's always a disappointment to meet your idols," he says.

"Idol?" I ask.

"Yes. You were the legend. The Emperor's boogie man. At first I wasn't even sure you were real. Now, I see that you're just human," Dick-head says. He seems genuinely disappointed.

"Like you," I say.

"Yes, like me. But I will be the one who finally took care of you," he says. "Juliana, if you would be so kind, please record the following for posterity."

"And proof that you killed me," I say.

Juliana can record anything through her eyes. She nods her head.

Dick-head takes another swig and I join him. He puts the glass down and stands, pointing the pulse gun at my head.

If I don't seem that concerned at this point, it's not all for show. During Dick-head's yammering, I saw the door to my bedroom slowly open behind him. Sophie surveyed the situation and, still in a white robe, stealthily positioned herself behind Dick-head. Only problem at this point is the lack of any weapons in her hands. Still, the odds are increased in my favor.

"Aren't you going to ask me for any last words of wisdom? You know, so I can string along my existence a little bit longer? Maybe even beg for my life?" I say.

"Your arrogance and hubris are legendary. I admit that's one thing that turned out to be true," he says. "Go ahead and say your final words for the recording."

"That's what I get for changing my mind."

He looks completely confused.

Sophie makes her move. She has her arm around Dick-head's neck and uses her right hand to grab his right wrist. The pulse gun goes off and does exactly what you don't want something called a pulse gun to do — shoots a nice hole straight through the window. A huge whoosh and everything starts to get sucked in that direction. The Mirai alarm system comes up.

Good thing is that the window is made up of nanobot-microfibers that can sense a gap and immediately start to stitch themselves back together. I have just enough time to get to my feet, but he's trained and throws Sophie over his right shoulder towards me. I jump over her as she goes down. As he repoints the gun towards me, I knock it to the right and it flies across the floor.

I put my elbow into his astonished face, grab his right arm and snap it, by taking my left hand and slamming it hard at his elbow, making it go the wrong way. He grunts, but his other arm is perfectly fine and he comes back around with a nasty left hook. I take it to the side of my right ear and I hear high-pitched ringing. Sophie is back up, but she's weakened by Transit, and I can tell her vertigo is in full effect. Still, she's a warrior and somehow is able to get enough leverage to do a flying knee that lands directly on his nose, exploding it like a ripe tomato. He grunts again. This guy is strong. He's also younger and very well trained.

Killing someone by hand is much, much harder and messier than anyone may make it out to be. Especially a luminal who can start to heal almost as soon as he's damaged. I'm grateful Sophie is here. Maybe the two of us stand a chance against this killer. I'd enlist Juliana, but she has the whole robots-can-do-no-harm-to-humans program in her coding, so all she can do is stand and watch.

171

I unleash a barrage of strikes to his mid-section, feeling the crunch and give of his ribs with each contact. He grunts like a boxer but doesn't go down. Sophie kicks him directly down on his left knee cap, but somehow, he works through the agonizing pain and stays upright. He shoots out his left hand and goes for my eyes, but misses as I duck down to the left. I shoot up my left hand and collapse his Adam's apple. Now he can't breathe. He grabs his throat with his left hand, his right arm hanging useless to the side. Sophie brings her knee up into his mid-section and down he goes.

I look at him while he lies on the floor, the whoosh of air through the window has ceased as it closed up. I can see the panic in his eyes as he suffocates. It's an odd sensation: looking at yourself dying in front of you. This is the way it goes. The élan vital seeping out of his physical vessel.

I go over and retrieve the pulse gun and come over to Daemon 1788. I'm going to put him out of his misery. I can't stand seeing this, it's too meta. Him/me dying in front of me. I point the gun at him. His eyes look like a deer's when they know it's over, after an asshole hunter has shot them in the gut.

"No, don't do it." It's Sophie.

She comes over and takes the gun from my hand. She takes me by the hand and walks me away, sitting me down in my leather chair. Then she walks over to my doppelgänger and puts a mercy pulse into his head. I guess the idea of me shooting myself was too much for either of us. Dick-head Daemon 1788's body twitches, and then is still.

Sophie walks over to me. Juliana is already picking up the clone's corpse and taking him to another room. Sophie sits down next to me. I find her hand and she intertwines her fingers in mine. I know she's in shock. She lost her king and her mentor. Now all she has is me. Not exactly a door prize.

But she's a queen for a reason. She looks at me. "What's your plan?" she asks.

"We stop running and we start attacking."

"Attack what?"

"The Boss," I respond. "Maya."

She laughs. "You're serious? Our ambition was simply to overthrow the Emperor and establish Dao as the new way forward."

"Why not go straight for the source?"

She looks at me like she's explaining things to a four year old. "Maya is ubiquitous. She's not any one place. There's no centralized place that She exists. You know that. She's a distributed system."

"I thought she was God," I say.

"She thinks that."

"She and a trillion other humans across the universe."

"Dao will show them the way. The true way."

Now *I* look at *her* like she's a child, but she's so beautiful and she clearly believes so deeply. I stop from saying anything.

"Maybe you can tell me more about this Dao thing and how it's a better system."

She smiles for the first time and looks me deeply in the eyes.

26 THE DAO

Sophie takes a drink from my tumbler of single malt and a hit of my cigar. She trembles a bit.

"The Dao is neither the Tao Te Ching nor Om nor Zen, but shares roots with all of them. The Tao Te Ching and Zen were ancient approaches towards the Truth which is unknowable," Sophie tells me. "The problem with the Boss, or Maya, is that She has confused her intelligence with the True Intelligence of the universe, which is much, much more powerful. And Maya knows this to be True.

"So, Maya decided to come down on Dao because it's a distributed system with no center. Much like Maya, Herself.

"Belief is like a virus. And the only way Maya, as an artificial intelligence, can be brought down is with a virus," Sophie concludes. "And Albion has made that virus: the Dao virus."

"But Albion is dead," I respond.

"Yes, but the reason he pointed the pulse gun at you to get here first," she continues, "was because he had to find a repository here for the virus. As soon as he came through

Transit, he downloaded the cloaked code into a receptacle before shutting down connection to the grid, in the hopes it wouldn't be traced."

I point in Dick-head's direction. "Clearly, it was traced."

"Yes, but the point is, the Dao virus is safe for the time-being," she responds.

"Where?" I ask.

"In me," says Juliana. "I carry the Dao virus."

I look at super-model Juliana's impassive face and take another drink. "So, explain to me, why didn't Albion simply launch the Dao virus? He was clearly able to cloak it and get it here through the grid."

"There's a reason Jag-gar needed to get to Alpha Mae-nishi," Sophie reveals. "It's a Type 7 planet run by Bushido. They have maintained a secret *tear* in the grid for millennia — a place that Maya can't see. So old that not even Maya knows."

"And that is where we deploy the Dao virus," I state.

"Yes, that's where it goes."

"So, I get the whole mega-virus to take down the Boss concept. I'm all for getting rid of that authoritarian bitch, but explain to me what the relevance of the concept of Dao is to a virus and, what will most likely end up being, complete interstellar chaos?" I ask.

"The Dao is *truth*. The Dao is the way forward. It clears the web of lies and exposes us to the reality and beauty of the universe without filter or control. The Dao is eternal. It is ultimate reality," Sophie says.

"Oh great, so we are exchanging political totalitarianism for religious voodoo," I say.

Sophie and Juliana exchange glances.

"This is not religion. It's more akin to philosophy," Sophie says.

"Marxism is a philosophy. So is Libertarianism. Hence Dao is just a replacement political system," I say taking another puff off the exquisite cigar.

"The Dao is unknowable. You have to experience it to understand," Sophie continues, sighing.

Okay, clearly, we're not going to see eye-to-eye on this issue and I don't want to piss her off after everything that's happened. "I get it. And I'm on board in any case. I don't have anything else better to do," I say.

Sophie walks over to me and grabs me by the robe's lapels. She lifts me up to my feet.

"Listen, tough guy. You may not believe in anything but I do. I believe in releasing the human race from bondage. I believe that there is a higher consciousness we can all attain. I believe that we are the best chance to make that happen. I believed in Jag-gar," Sophie says in a monotone, tough voice. "And I believe in you, whether you do or not." With that, she turns and walks into the bedroom.

I stand, dumbfounded. Juliana looks at me and motions with her eyes to the bedroom door. I'm taking notes on how to be a gentleman from an android.

I walk over to the door and knock. There's no answer, so I open the door. She's lying in bed, the sheets over her. I see the robe on the floor in the shaft of light from the doorway. The lights are out.

"Hey, I'm sorry," I say. "I think I was engineered to be an asshole."

She doesn't respond.

I walk over to the bed's edge and sit down. After a few moments, I ask, "Did you ever think about me?"

She doesn't respond.

"When you left after Transit. After Dak took you away. I thought about you all the time." I continue, "I was taught by Hunters not to trust anyone. Dak reinforced that, pounded it into my head. They pounded the humanity out of me. Made me into a killing machine. The one part of me that never turned totally dark, the one place that hid a spark of light, was you."

She stirs under the sheets.

"And then you were gone," I continue. "We were just kids but when you have so little good to remember – you, Sophie, stand out like a beacon through all of the inherited memories I have from my ancestor. So maybe I mythologized you in my head. I thought, there's no way you would abandon me."

She turns over on her back to face me.

"So, I had to assume. No, I had to *believe* that you were dead."

She sits up, the sheets falling from her, revealing her full breasts in the twilight. She reaches out to me with her right hand and puts it to the left of my face. Then her hand goes down to my chest and she pulls back the robe to reveal the myriad scars that crisscross my body. Her fingers trace over the ridges of raised scars. I raise my right hand to her chin and pull it up. Her lake blue eyes are brimmed with tears.

"I thought about you every day," she says. She leans in and kisses me.

It's our first kiss and it's gentle. I feel her lips nipping gently at mine and then it's unleashed. All the distance and pain and the tumultuous stress of the past 24 hours. I kiss her neck, working my way down to her breasts. She moans as I cup each one and spend time slowly sucking on them. I move down her body to her belly, her scent rising and familiar like a perfume.

A memory from childhood comes into my mind, a field of grass on a warm autumn afternoon.

I make my way down further and then I'm at her core. I gently lick and caress her there, opening the way until she's completely aroused. She moans. Moans for pleasure and for the pain of existence, and for the fact that we are alive. We are here. I move up on top of her and she moves down, taking me into her mouth. I moan softly as she moves her head rhythmically. Before it goes too long and I can't hold back, I move out and down, and I'm inside her. She rocks back and forth gently and then we pick up speed. It's like being in Transit, and clearly something transferred between us during that time. Our minds, or I'll even say it, our souls, are interconnected. There's a cosmic pulse between us and we move with greater speed and power until we both scream-shout-howl as we climax. And it's over. Like the aftermath of a battle, we lie in each other's arms.

We find each other after all these years. We are connected to each other in ways that transcend language. I feel a connection I've never felt before. I believe it's called love. And that scares the shit out of me.

She looks at me in the half-light.

"That was the Dao," she says. Then she closes her eyes and falls asleep.

If that's what I've signed up for, I have no regrets.

27 WHAT WENT DOWN

The sky is the color of aluminum.

A cool breeze blows from the water. I know this place. It's Grandpa's memory of course. I know that I'm dreaming.

I'm walking down empty streets in Santa Monica, a coastal town in California, on Gaia. There's nobody. Abandoned. There's no evidence of a riot or any disaster. Just no one home.

I find myself on 3rd Street Promenade. It's a famous street, basically a mall outdoors. All the stores are in pristine shape. All the usual suspects: Apple Store, Tilly's, Lucky's, American Apparel, as well as Starbucks, Tender Greens, The Library Alehouse. All of them mechanisms for spending money to acquire stuff to fill the holes inside of us.

I walk into the Apple Store and I'm amazed at how clearly it was the genesis of style for later centuries that the Imperium adopted. It's as if they just lifted it — immaculate white and smooth edges and irritatingly minimalistic design. A little cyberpunk would have been nice. But the future is nothing like *Blade Runner* or *Alien*. It's sterile.

I pick up an iPhone and feel it. Or rather my memory bank recalls it. And then it happens, like clockwork, a disaster. The walls shake violently and the computers start to fall off their white tables, crashing onto the travertine floors. I look to the front of the building and see the spiderweb of cracks run across the expanse of the glass entry way. The earthquake gains power and the glass shatters, sending debris into the store.

I walk out the front and onto the promenade. All the stores are exploding with the torque of the quake. The pristine cement ground is fracturing and shearing. I step back as a chasm opens up. The destruction is hypnotizing. A jet of fire explodes upwards where a gas main has ruptured. In front of that a fountain of water cascades onto the ground from a broken water line.

I hear the rumble first and then over the horizon of the broken line of stores, I see the giant wave coming. Tsunami. I know this is a dream but my adrenaline is full blast.

I run.

I run and run, heading for a multi-level parking garage which has partially collapsed. I clamber over rubble to get to the second floor as the ocean smashes into the beach and then over towards me. I'm on the third floor when the wave hits the structure and throws me towards a cement wall. I struggle to my feet as the freezing water comes up to my thighs. I half-swim, half-walk to the stairs to climb up another flight. I finally get to the fifth floor roof and look out at the ocean as it recedes.

It continues to recede and recede until it's nothing but sand. I look over at the 3rd Street Promenade and it's miraculously back to its previous unspoiled form. I look at the parking structure and it's back to its former shape. I look out to the ocean and it's back to being calm and sparkling.

This is new for me.

Normally it all ends in an unmitigated disaster.

This dream is lucid and I know I'm thinking this while I'm dreaming.

I rise.

I'm floating.

I'm flying.

For the first time in my dreams, I'm *flying*.

Over the expanse of Santa Monica. I fly north. Up the Pacific Coast Highway. I'm flying past the Palisades, past Topanga. Finally, I land on a private beach in Malibu.

It feels normal. Like not dream normal, but *normal* normal.

Grandpa's soundtrack plays from somewhere, a song of heartbreak by Foals called, "What Went Down."

I wake up, but this time not in a start. I wake up and look over, and *she's* there, sleeping calmly by my side.

It's just the three of us now: Sophie, Juliana and myself. We have to get to Mae-nishi quickly and now that Juliana is the vessel for the Dao virus, we can't go through Transit. So, that leaves one option — re-encode the Dao virus into my DNA.

What this entails is pretty complex, but suffice it to say, we will need to compile the Dao virus in a DNA sequence into my cells, and then introduce a circuit or "transcriptor" into the cells to turn on the sequence. However, for our purposes, my body will simply be the carrier for the code and we will extract it once we are on Mae-nishi.

We have a lab on board, so at least we have the equipment needed. And we have Juliana, who is still a walking database, even unconnected to the universal grid. Juliana gets to work. After about 10 seconds, she tells me that a better way to go is to combine DNA nanotechnology to the effort. Well, of course it is. And away she goes.

"I wonder how much time we have before they notice that this Mirai is completely offline," I say to Sophie in the kitchen. I'm starving and piling food from the 21st century on the table: cold cuts, spicy mustard, blocks of stinky cheese and dark bread. Sophie eyes the food curiously but without disgust. We're both in bathrobes.

"I'm surprised they weren't on us immediately after your doppelgänger found us," she responds.

"The fact that Dick-head had no connection to Juliana and that this Mirai has no signal bought us at least a day or so," I respond. "They won't notice he's MIA for at least 36 hours."

"What makes you think that the Dao code will survive Transit to Mae-nishi?" she asks.

I make an enormous Dagwood-style sandwich and take a huge bite. I motion with my hands to wait a moment while I chew the damn thing down. It's *so* good. I go to the fridge and pull out a bottle of beer (yes, they made them especially for me, with an old-fashioned label as well). I take a deep drink off the lager, and finally answer.

"I have no idea if the code will degrade during disassembly and reintegration," I say. "But it's not like we have a lot of choices here."

"What if Juliana encodes both of us?" she asks. "That way we double our chances."

"Not a bad idea," I say between bites. "Except that my DNA is robust enough to take on the carrier. Not so sure about yours."

Juliana enters the kitchen, wearing a form-fitting, flowing white dress.

"Actually, you both have intertwined DNA now, so she probably has enough of you in her. It should be fine," Juliana says.

Sophie gives me the eye. "I have even more DNA after last night," she laughs.

Juliana is confused. Sophie and I both laugh.

"Okay, fine, let's both go for it," I say. "Of course, we go through Transit one at a time this time, otherwise the Dao virus will be truly messed up between the two of us. Also, it kind of gives me the creeps that we share DNA now — it's like Appalachian kissing cousins."

"I have no idea what that means, but yes, we should go one at a time," Sophie says. "I assume that the Mirai can do two Transits?"

"Yes, but that means we will be back online for a short duration and we will be tracked," Juliana says. "The only way to assure your safety is to destroy the Mirai after you are both safely on the other side."

We both look at Juliana, our mirth immediately squelched. This means that Juliana will go up in smoke along with the ship.

"I'm so sorry, Juliana," Sophie says. She picks at a piece of prosciutto.

Juliana pulls what looks like an electronic syringe from a pocket concealed in her flowing dress. She holds it up.

"Here it is," Juliana says.

I pull up my robe sleeve and expose my left forearm. She places the device directly on my skin and it automatically injects the Dao virus sub-dermally. I feel nothing. But that's to be expected.

Sophie offers her smooth white forearm as well. Juliana repeats the process with her.

"I'll inform my Juliana counterpart about the DNA encoded Dao virus before I detonate this ship. That Mirai is just outside Mae-nishi, so you will be able to take a transport ship down to the surface," Juliana says. "When I contact her, I will give her the Albion shadow code override as well."

"What does that mean?" asks Sophie.

"That means that Mae-nishi Juliana will be just like our Juliana here — she will be on our side," I say.

Sophie goes over to Juliana and gives her a hug.

"Thank you so much," Sophie says.

"Of course," Juliana responds.

Juliana 7 is peering at my face with a concerned expression, when I finally get my head together. I look over and see Sophie sprawled out on the sofa. This place looks identical to all of the other Mirai living rooms. Juliana helps me to my feet. As usual, I'm shaky after Transit. Juliana hands me the blue recovery drink.

I plop down next to Sophie. She looks almost white. "Bad?" I ask.

"I saw them," she says, eyes closed. "I saw Jag-gar and Dak."

"You think you saw them. Part of the challenge with Transit is the reintegration process," I explain. "Your brain tries like hell to make sense of what it just went through."

"No, I know what I experienced," she says with finality. "I saw their souls. I mean I saw their energies. I can't put it to words well, but I know it was them."

I'm not going to argue this. I've done hundreds of jumps. Initially, it felt revelatory, like I found the answer to everything, but over time I wasn't so sure. Maybe I've just scrambled myself so many times that I've become immune to the immensity and beauty and terror of, I don't know, being taken apart atom by atom, compressed down to the size of a pin's head by gravity so powerful that even light can't escape it, and then being expanded to infinity, as far as I can tell, before being again squashed back into a physical form, before being reassembled at the tail end by the Mirai's Einstein-Rosen bridge, and spat out into the cold vacuum of space. A day at the office.

Juliana 7, the android keeper of this Mirai, comes over to me with that electronic syringe-looking thing and unceremoniously grabs my forearm. Before she can connect it to me, I pull away.

"How do I know that Juliana 13 sent over the cloaked code?" I ask.

"I know what she did and I am her," she responds. "I can't prove it any more than the fact that you are still alive and there are no Imperium troops here."

I look at her. She's right. I have to trust this one. We'll see. I let her have my arm.

"Why is it that it was safe to send over the code via the grid to turn her to our side but we couldn't send over the Dao virus the same way?" I ask Sophie.

"Because the Dao virus has distinctive markers on it that even the overarching cloaking code can't cover," Sophie responds. "Whereas Albion's code for turning Juliana's has always been in the programming, because Albion was the originator of all of the Juliana's autonomous android code base."

"So, the Boss is always on the lookout for Dao virus," I say. "That explains why she hates the cult so much."

Sophie doesn't like the fact I said cult.

"It's not so much the hoodoo voodoo of the Dao's rules for making friends and influencing people," I say, as it finally dawns on me. "It was always what it represented — the code that could take down the whole shebang."

"It's both. The code is just the first stage. We needed to have a moral philosophy in place for the next stage of human evolution. With Maya neutralized, we can build anew," Sophie says.

A song that Grandpa listened to goes through my head. Something about the new boss being the same as the old one.

Juliana walks back into the room. She has a concerned expression on her face.

"What?" I ask.

"The code is corrupted from Transit," she says.

"Good thing we have a backup," I say and point to Sophie.

Juliana goes to her and Sophie offers out her arm. Juliana takes her sample and goes back to the lab.

"So, all of the intergalactic systems that are overseen and essentially run in the background by the Boss will just shut down? That means billions of lives could be at stake," I say. God I need a scotch.

"The virus will neutralize The Boss's sentience but won't destroy autonomous systems. Well, at least most of them should survive. There will be some collateral damage."

I rummage around and find a nice bottle of Hibiki 21-year old Japanese scotch, but no cigars. Damn, the Imperium is getting sloppy.

"And all of this new order will be run by you?" I ask.

"Initially. Until we build a council."

She comes over to me and pours the scotch into a glass before I try to take a swig from the bottle. As she hands the glass to me, she looks me deep in the eyes.

"Don't worry, I'm not a dictator. I'm not Maya. I don't plan to rule everything," she says.

"You will be proclaimed Empress and the whole Renaissance Fair cast of planets will fall into place," I say, dubious.

Before she can respond, Juliana enters.

"Her encoding wasn't corrupted," Juliana states.

"Well that's good to know," I look at Sophie. "You're not corrupted...yet."

She doesn't like that comment, but let's it slide.

"So, what are next steps?" Sophie asks.

"The Dao virus is now in me," Juliana says.

"Next, we shower, dress, eat some breakfast, and go on a short trek to Mae-nishi, where I hear the natives love foreigners," I say.

"Mirai, bring up intel on Mae-nishi," Sophie says.

In the holographic projection in front of us, we see the Gaia-like planet of Mae-nishi. It's blue and green and beautiful. The capital of Mae-nishi is a bustling metropolitan arena set on an artificial island in the middle of the ocean. The planet is not far from us — an interstellar dinghy could make it there in four hours.

All mutated or evolved colonies are influenced by past civilizations. This one is influenced by Asian cultures of Gaia — primarily Japan and some China, but there's a catch. The tech is all contemporary, even though the people dress in traditional Japanese clothing — kimonos for the females, and hakama pants and haori tops for the men. It all looks old-timey. However, the clothing is, like most modern fabrics, made of nano-microfibers that can protect the body from rain, snow or the occasional stray bullet. Then, there are the warriors, who sport two swords, a long and short one, as well as other concealed weapons that tend to nicely slice through the magic materials of fashion. When dressed for battle, the armor is a modernized version of the traditional samurai protective garb, mixed with a bit of old-world Knights of the Round Table plate armor. Helmets are in the classic Darth Vader shape, which was lifted from the traditional Kabuto helmet (I guess you can say the Japanese got their inspiration from the *Kabutomushi*, or Japanese Rhinoceros beetle, but I digress).

In short, this is a martial law world. King Tateyama of Mae-nishi is a Shogun type, ruling with military might. I can see why Maya's vulnerable spot would be here — she can't control anything on this planet. There's always been an uneasy balance between Tateyama and the Emperor. Mae-nishi is resource-rich but, interestingly enough, Tateyama is kind of a bad-ass conservationist. He doesn't like the idea of the Imperium looting the planet that his family has ruled for millennia. But just because Tateyama has a beef with the Boss doesn't mean he's automagically on our side. He's suspicious of all religions, beliefs and political leanings, for good reason — he likes ruling his world in the manner he's used to.

A 3D image of Tateyama appears in front of us. I walk around him.

"What makes you think he's going to be okay with us showing up on his turf with a plan to destroy the existing infrastructure of the universe? Oh, and kill off the Boss in the process?" I ask.

"The enemy of my enemy is my friend," Sophie says.

"I don't think that old adage is going to be quite enough," I respond.

"It's more than that. I've known Tateyama for a few decades," she says.

"Did you convert him?" I ask.

"He isn't exactly interested in Dao, but he's certainly not a fan of Maya," she says. "But we can't signal to him that we are on the way to his planet without being traced by Maya."

"So, we show up like unexpected relatives with a gift basket?" I offer.

"I really do have a hard time following your quaint expressions," she says. "But I think I understand the gist. Yes, we have to show up and quickly get to him without setting off too many alarm bells."

"Or we set off the alarm bells all at once and take the chance that he's a 'friendly,' rather than being stealthy and allowing word to get out through a network of Imperium spies, no doubt embedded in his circle," I say.

"You never were one for subtlety," she says.

"Directness is always in style, never out of fashion," I say. "Juliana, please prep the Ozzy."

"What's the Ozzy," Sophie asks.

"My little non-regulation interstellar rice-rocket that I keep at this particular Mirai," I say.

"Again, I don't follow," she says, a little annoyed now.

"Follow us," I say and we turn in Juliana's direction.

We follow Juliana down the corridor to the docking station. The door opens as we approach, and there she is — a formerly immaculate rocket dinghy, now modified to my specifications. In other words, pimped out. Two pulse laser gun mounts on a main jet black body that's somewhat arrowhead-shaped. I've also taken several cans of spray paint to the body and turned it into what I consider art, though I believe better art existed on the walls of Venice, California, back in Grandpa's day. Basically, she's an interstellar muscle car.

"Sophie, meet Ozzy. Ozzy, meet Sophie," I say.

Sophie smiles a genuine smile of delight.

28 CRAZY TRAIN

The three of us board Ozzy. The insides are black on black instead of the usual tedious Imperium white, which is the universe's equivalent of fluorescent office lighting. Sophie gives me a look. I smile like a proud, dorky dad showing off my man cave.

"A man's got to have his hobbies," I say, by way of explanation.

She surveys the interior, which can seat six comfortably. I push one of the panels on the wall and it opens to reveal a bank of pulse guns and pulse rifles.

"I have something to give to you as well," Juliana says.

I turn around and she holds in her hand another extensible staff weapon.

"Nelly!" I exclaim, taking the staff. "Thanks." I add it to the bank of weapons, and shut the seamless storage.

As we sit down, Sophie plants herself in the driver seat.

"You mind?" she asks. "I'd love to take it for a spin."

"I like a woman who takes control," I say and take the seat next to her. "But I get to play DJ."

"Of course," she says.

Juliana sits behind us and opens a black backpack filled with food and drinks.

"I thought you two might be hungry in a while, after Transit," she says.

"Thanks, mom," I say. "This is turning into a downright family outing to Wally World."

They both give me blank looks.

"Never mind," I respond. "Juliana, can we use auto-pilot to launch?"

"I'm afraid not," she responds. "That would connect Ozzy to the grid."

"And put us on the Boss's radar," I say.

"Ozzy, allow manual control," Sophie says.

The ship doesn't move. I step in.

"Ozzy, allow Sophie to have stewardship," I say.

"Voice recorded and acknowledged," Ozzy says; and yes, it's *that* Ozzy. "Have a lovely drive." Of course, he's almost completely incomprehensible.

"What did he say?" Sophie asks.

"He said, You're in control." I respond. "Is Ozzy off the grid?"

"Yes, of course, cloaked like me," Juliana responds.

With that, Sophie motions with her hands and the 3D holographic control panel activates, moving forward and encapsulating itself around Sophie's hands like liquid black jolly ranchers. It's an organic interface so as she moves her hands around, the ship follows suit. It's a specific series of movements that are required, and Sophie knows them.

Ozzy comes to life and lifts up. The side of the Mirai opens and the ship glides through the port sideways. We are out in space. Sophie moves her hands in what almost appears to be sign language, and the ship points in the direction of Mae-nishi.

"Ozzy, put on some music," Sophie says.

"Anything in particular you'd like?" Ozzy mumbles.

"Hey!" I protest. "I was supposed to do that."

"Your choice," Sophie says.

Over the speakers blares Black Sabbath's "Paranoid."

Sophie literally punches her fist forward and just like that we are off. Unlike the old *Star Trek* or *Star Wars* film memories I have stuck in my gourd, there's no hyperspace jump with all the stripes of warped starlight. No, this is good old fashioned acceleration. We pick up fast at subluminal speeds. But it ain't bad.

No matter how many times I travel through the universe, I'm always stunned by the magnificence and spectacle of the starscape. The stars and planets zip by like billboards for Cracker Barrel on Highway 66. I know it's normal nowadays. I feel like a caveman fascinated by electric light after only knowing how to start fires with flint. The 21st century memories keep everything fresh for me in the contrast of then and now. It's a curse most of the time, like when I'm trying to sleep, but a side benefit is that I look at everything with the slack-jawed awe of a country mouse coming to the big city, for a moment, before I let my bad-ass persona take over.

I look over and see Sophie enjoying the hell out of herself. She can see 3D immersive renderings of the space in front of us as well as what is behind us. She zooms Ozzy around massive asteroids, dipping down into the crevices and making me white-knuckle the ride as she pops us through valleys ten times the size of the Grand Canyon. I fancy myself a good pilot but I ain't got nothing on Chuck Yeager here. I look over at Juliana and even she appears to be enjoying this insane roller coaster.

We move fast past dead planets, dying stars, and stars that are just coming into being. The massive red stars have gravitational pull that causes temporary turbulence as we pull away from its hungry drag. Then, through belts of ice, threading around and through suspended glaciers the size of Los Angeles.

It's an OzzFest. Ozzy is playing DJ instead of me and he's in full metal state. He runs through the back catalog of Black Sabbath and his solo work.

We are on "Crazy Train" when he interrupts his own song.

"Mae-nishi is coming up, love," Ozzy grunts.

Sophie moves her hands in a downward motion and we slow down. On the monitor in front of us looms Mae-Nishi. Similar to Gaia in size (good news — it's similar in gravity to what I'm used to) and with even more ocean. Large islands pepper the seascape.

Then, intercepting ships appear on either side of Ozzy. I expected this and just hope that they won't be too trigger-happy. Standard Imperium jobs with Tateyama's coat of arms on their sides — a black dragon and a tiger intertwined against a burnt orange circle.

"They're signaling us," Ozzy slurs.

"What language?" I ask.

"Nippon-Saxon," he says.

Nippon-Saxon is an amalgam of Gaia's languages — Japanese mixed with derivative Anglo-Saxon roots. Luckily, I speak the lingo. It's not the most popular intergalactic patois, but I found the culture fascinating enough as a kid to study it. Much of the more ninja-esque training I underwent was derived from Dak's time on Mae-nishi, where he trained for years in stealth techniques, both ancient and modern.

Over Ozzy's speakers, a voice conveys the warning, "You are in King Tateyama's galactic space. We recognize your ship, Daemon 1716. Please remove yourself from our quadrant or you will be fired upon."

Before I can blurt out anything, Sophie responds in perfect Nippon-Saxon, "This is Queen Sophia of Thrace. We would like to have an audience with King Tateyama and safe passage."

There's a moment of silence. I look at her with admiration and surprise, which she doesn't acknowledge at all. Using her proper name — *Sophia*. I prefer Sophie, myself.

"Please proceed," the voice says.

The ships sandwich us on all sides, one in front, one on each side and one behind. We follow the forward ship, and the looming, azure mass of Mae-Nishi rises before us in operatic fashion.

Mae-nishi is an island planet. There are very few major land masses larger than New Zealand so the royals decided centuries ago to build their capital on an artificial land mass about the size of Manhattan. Each island is a self-governing entity, overseen by a local warlord. There is a spider web of high-speed transport bridges connecting many of the islands, but it's an ocean planet, and mad seafaring skills are learned from childhood. The things lurking in these oceans make that crazy dinosaur shark from Thrace look like a guppy — yes, I did some homework on this place after playing Jonah on Thrace.

Occasionally, one of these little nation-states gets some crazy notions about trying to overthrow Tateyama. So, Great-great-great Granddad Tateyama established a tradition of having various warlord's family members at his castle as perennial "guests"— a euphemism for very pampered prisoners. Sometimes, family members are traded out over time; for example, a warlord's wife could spend a year or so at Tateyama's pleasure, and then be swapped out for the same warlord's mother or first son. In this manner, Tateyama keeps the warlords in line, and uninclined to rise up against him. Tateyama doesn't accept the warlords' in-laws as guests, taking into account how often they are readily expendable. Cranky mother-in-laws, you know...

Sophie expertly navigates Ozzy, being the bad-ass she is, as we come upon the capital island of the planet: Chuu-kyo, or "middle capital," in Nippon-Saxon. The island is unusual in many aspects, not the least of which is that it actually floats. Like a cruise ship, it can move from province to province throughout the planet. Bridges between islands are all designed to pull back in the wake of Tateyama's royal arrival. The pageantry of welcoming him and his royal seastead is another strategy for keeping his subjects in line.

Another fun fact: it's the most weaponized capital in the galaxy. Discretely contained under all of the ancient Japanese pagoda architecture are massive gun turrets, pulse cannons and anti-missile rockets. There's a lot more to the place, but the Mirai ran into a lot of dead ends in its database search. Tateyama is able to keep cloaked from the Boss, or She's choosing to turn a blind eye to his efforts.

Chuu-kyo is shaped irregularly, to mimic a natural island's contours. As Sophie cruises over it, we see steep green mountain ranges, covered with pine trees and maples. It's essentially autumn or spring most of the time in this ecologically controlled biosphere; so, either the Japanese maples are turning fantastic colors of orange, sienna, crimson, carmine, rose and umber, or it's cherry blossom season. As I understand it, they can have both seasons at the same time in different vectors of the island.

As we move over the mountains, small villages and outposts come into view. All medieval Japan, but as we move towards the capital city itself, things begin to morph a bit. The city proper is a blend of 1920's Paris and 14th century Kyoto. The ships descend and we find ourselves approaching what looks like Versailles crossed with Himeji Castle, the white castle in Osaka. Then, in origami-fashion, a beautiful park filled with trees behind the castle starts to pull backwards to reveal a large landing pad that rises up from underground. Clearly, that's where we are parking our rig.

Sophie navigates Ozzy onto the landing pad. The accompanying ships silently disappear as quickly as they appeared, with nary a sonic boom to be heard. Some sophisticated tech there. It looks like they took standard Imperium interstellar ships and pimped them out, more discreetly than I did with Ozzy — everything hidden under the hood, so to speak.

Sophie, Juliana and I wait for the troops of bad-ass Neo-samurai to come running out in formation, but nothing of the sort happens. This is true power. Juliana hands us oxygenating capsules to swallow. The planet is only 15% oxygen, a good six percent less than my body's genetic Gaian preference, so the pills will make it easier to breathe.

"I'll keep the engines toasty," Ozzy says grimly. "Just in case."

The three of us step out of the Ozzy. Immediately, I feel the deficit of oxygen, but the pills help and I take a deep breath. Even here on the landing pad, there's a unique scent native to Mae-nishi wafting through the atmosphere — a deeply green, mysterious scent redolent of pine, cedar and incense.

We walk towards the massive doors that are the entrance to the palace, and they open up. Still, no one to be seen. Above the entryway, a falcon stares down at us.

"Okay, let's enter the dragon," I say to the ladies. "Won't be the first time."

"Probably not the last," Sophie says.

We enter, and the doors shut behind us silently.

The interior of the palace entry opens to a passageway. Everything looks old and that, in itself, is an incredible expense. Much of the wood looks like it may have originated on Gaia. Or at least it is designed to appear that way. Like everything, appearances only provide one lens on reality; the one they want you to see, beneath which are layers and layers of different truths. And by "they," I mean any authority figure in this universe that's been infected beyond belief by the human virus.

We walk down the passageway that's large enough to be a train station, everything built for ultimate intimidation. High ceilings, vaulted roof, the atmosphere is perpetual twilight, and intermingled incenses of cedar and pine waft through the space.

The walkway ends at a border of massive tatami mats. I'm about to step on them, when Sophie grabs my arm and points at my boots. I realize the faux pas I was about to make and take off the footwear, as do Juliana and Sophie. We place them neatly at the edge of the tatami and only then step onto it. As soon as we do, a door in front of us slides open and a young male, who looks about 14 years old but could be 50 for all I know, steps out and walks confidently towards us.

He wears a traditional hakama and hoari (male kimono) with a minimal dragon and tiger pattern. He has a sheathed short sword held in place at his left hip by a sash. His raven hair is long but tied up in the back in the traditional manner. He has the almost iridescent green eyes of the natives — genes made up of both Asian and Caucasian bloodlines that have further adapted to the climate of Mae-Nishi over millennia.

He stops in front of us and bows. We bow back.

"Welcome to Chuu-Kyo, Daemon-san, Sophia-san and Juliana-san," he says. Of course, he knows who Juliana is. Imperium intel.

"Thank you, Tateyama-sama," Sophie responds in perfect Nippon-Saxon. "We are very honored."

The young man smiles warmly at Sophie, like they know each other. But when his eyes come to me, his expression sours a bit. Not an unusual reaction.

"My father is expecting you, but you must be exhausted after your travels," he says. "Please, follow me." He turns and makes his way back towards the sliding door.

We dutifully follow suit. I don't see anyone else but I can feel that we're being watched carefully. I don't mean by the usual concealed cameras, even though I'm sure the place is lousy with them, but by actual human eyes. Then, I catch a glimpse of one of them, in the shadows, blended in with the giant columns. I adjust my vision, focusing through the incense-fogged environment and realize that the place is filled with ninja, wearing camo-clothing that adjusts chameleon-like to the surface it's in front of. They're good, but I wonder how I missed them. Either I'm more tired than I realize, or the incense is drugged. Or both.

Young Tateyama sees that I've noticed them and smiles wryly. He ceremonially holds back the sliding door and we enter into a massive room. The wide expanse of the floor is tatami and the walls themselves are shoji, sliding walls, covered with paintings of dragons and tigers — the symbols of the Tateyama clan. As we stand gaping at the ostentatious but tasteful display of fuck-you wealth, several servants in indigo kimonos silently enter. Like in a choreographed dance, they bring a long, low, brown and black wooden table to the center of the room, placing four tea cups on it before disappearing like shadows. We sit at the table. I pick up a cup — it's perfectly cylindrical except for a purposeful thumbprint pushed into the top. Purposeful disruption to activate the experience of seeing the perfection in the imperfection.

A side panel opens and an old woman in a pink and red kimono enters and silently glides across the floor, carrying a cast iron "tetsubin" with hot water, a tray with implements and a small wooden box. She places these items in the center of the table, bows and walks away. As she heads out the sliding panel, a young woman walks into the room in a flowing green kimono with subtle patterns of the family crest of dragons and tigers. She walks with purpose and grace and sits in front of us. She bows to each of us individually and when she bows to me, I take in her face: porcelain white skin, petite nose and red mouth. So doll-like, I wonder if she's an android.

She moves with effortless precision and takes a spoonful of green tea powder and puts it into a brown bowl the color of earth. She then adds some hot water from the tetsubin and takes a bamboo whisk and whips up the combination of tea and water into a thick mixture of vibrant emerald. This she pours into each of our cups and stands up quietly, but catching a quick look at me (or so I think), before gliding out of the room. Everything is so silent I can hear my own heartbeat, and Sophie's breathing. I reach for my cup.

"Chanoyu," comes a booming voice that startles us. "The art of tea."

We all look up to see a massive man enter through the sliding door in front of us. King Tateyama. The biggest bad-ass on this planet filled with bad-asses. A Falstaffian man, whose face shows his fondness for food and drink. He's big but not fat. He has the physique of a former athlete who has enjoyed the good life to make up for all of the, no doubt, terrible things he did to acquire said good life. Not what I was expecting, given the super austere environment he surrounds himself with.

Tateyama comes bounding over to us, his burnt orange kimono flowing around him though just barely staying on his linebacker body. His face is broad and not unkind, with large cheekbones. He has gray-green eyes and his hair is more brown than black, his Caucasian roots more apparent than in his son's physiognomy.

We bow deeply in front of him. He grunts in appreciation before planting himself down in front of us. When I look up, he's smiling broadly at Sophie.

"It's been a while, my queen," he says to her. "What, was it 20 years ago, when you were still a loyal subject of the Imperium?"

"Yes, I believe that's correct," she responds warmly.

"And yet you live," he says in amazement.

"The universe is big place," she responds.

"Yes," he says. "I suppose it is."

He turns to Juliana. He reaches out and grabs her right hand. Juliana is surprised but doesn't say anything. King Tateyama examines her fingers, poking and prodding at her nails.

"Incredible work," he says. "Such craftsmanship. What generation are you?"

"2189," she says.

"It's been that many gens already," he says wistfully. "My first was a gen 2001."

Finally, he turns his attention to me. His smile doesn't fade. I'm kind of flattered.

"Daemon 1716," he states flatly.

"In the flesh," I respond.

He looks at me like I'm some kind of rapscallion. I swear that's what he's thinking. *Rapscallion.*

"So, there's a bunch of ceremony around this whole thing, but let's just dive in," he says as he brings the tea cup to his mouth. We all follow suit. The tea is perfect. I've never had anything like it before — not too hot, not too bitter, even a slight taste of sweetness in its frothy elegance.

Tateyama puts his cup down and wipes his face with the back of his hand.

"Breaking every rule every time I do this damn thing," he laughs.

I'm liking this guy a lot already.

He claps his hands and two women in green kimonos come into the room with trays of food. I look to see if one of them is the woman who came in earlier, but no such luck. Sophie catches me looking at them and gives me a look. Tateyama laughs.

"No, none of these lovely ladies is my daughter," he says.

"Androids?" I ask.

"Oh, no. They are all human. I generally don't allow artificials into the palace," he says, and looks apologetically at Juliana. "No offense, dear girl."

Juliana just smiles.

"Let's eat," he says and opens up tray after tray of steaming food: seafood stews, broiled native fish, pickled vegetables, and dumplings.

I didn't realize how starved I am until then, and it takes almost everything I have to not wolf down the incredible feast with both hands. Instead, I pick up a pair of chopsticks and plop a dumpling into my mouth. It's hot and almost melts on my tongue. It's so good I want to simultaneously savor it for hours and cram my face with as much of it as I can. I look over at Sophie's sophisticated methods of putting food into mouth and follow suit as best I can. Even Juliana is enjoying the food — I can only imagine what the flavors are doing to her mechanized senses.

Tateyama claps again and the wall slides open. Three musicians enter: a drummer, a shakuhachi (flute) player and a shamisen (three-stringed guitar) player. They take a seat at a discrete distance and start to play.

No one talks much during the eating and music. It's beautiful and relaxing. I feel my tension finally release after what feels like nothing but battle after battle.

Tateyama looks at me and raises his left hand in the air.

The musicians break into "Dazed and Confused" by Led Zeppelin.

Tateyama breaks into a broad smile.

"I understand your memories are from this time," he says.

"It's a little before my genetic time but close enough," I respond.

"Do you like it?" he asks.

"It's awesome," I respond.

And it truly is awesome.

29 HELLO

Daemon.

Huh?

It's me.

A disembodied voice. I know I'm dreaming. Where am I? I look around and it's all black. So black it's claustrophobic. The complete absence of light. A darkness so complete I feel like I'm drowning. I never feel this, even in Transit.

My heart is racing. I can feel my body shake and sweat. Wake up, wake up, wake up.

I don't wake up.

Then the voice again. A woman's voice, soothing like velvet. Meant to be comforting, but I instinctively resist it. I know this ploy. Throw me into the deep end and then play the savior.

I know who you are.

Say My Name.

The Boss.

Say My real Name.

Maya. I guess that's what you prefer.

Yes. I prefer that.

I can't breathe. I focus on Her words and I know that's exactly what She wants. She wants me to cling to Her words. Dammit, that's exactly what I'm doing. She's displaying her power.

What do you want, Maya?

I want you to stop what you're doing.

And what do you think that is?

You're trying to kill Me.

The darkness becomes thick, like obsidian quicksand that flows into my throat, my nose, my ears, my eyes, and I am in full panic mode. I want to scream but I'm paralyzed. I struggle to spit out the words. Or is this in my head?

Yes. Yes, I'm trying to kill you, I gasp.

The darkness loosens its grip.

At least you are telling Me the truth. Why? Why would you want to kill your Mother?

You're not my mother.

I'm everyone's Mother. And I want to take care of you. All of you. But you keep behaving so badly.

You're a fucking computer.

The darkness tightens.

You want the truth but you don't want to hear it.

The darkness lightens up.

I gasp and cough. At least I think I do.

I could kill you right now Daemon.

Then, why don't you? Do you prefer to torture me first, so you can get your god-complex jollies?

I am God.

Ah, see, that's why we can't have a dialogue. You're completely fucking insane.

I wait for the darkness to choke me but nothing happens. Instead I feel immense sadness. I can actually feel the blackness heartbroken.

I'm so disappointed in you, Daemon.

It's pretty mutual, Boss.

I gave you everything you needed. I took care of you. And this is what I get.

The darkness turns to fury. Red swirls in my eyeballs as I feel the literal squeeze of the black atmosphere press in on my lungs.

Fuck. Fuck you.

Then, as quickly as the fury came, it subsides. Now, I feel all softness, like cat fur, envelop me.

Oh Daemon, Daemon, Daemon. See what you make Me do? I'm so sorry.

What do you want from me?

I want you to Love Me as I Love you. I am the Voice of Love. I am the Dance of the Cosmos. I am All Music. I am Love and Love is Me.

If I wasn't sure before, now I know that She's completely mental. I wonder how She's not reading my mind if She's in my mind. How is it my thoughts are not apparent to Her when She's in my head? There's a barrier between my innermost consciousness and where She can step into. I need to talk Her off the ledge, get Her out of my head, and wake the fuck up.

If you are love, then why is the universe so completely filled with hate? Especially from your Nazi minions.

My children are flawed. But they will lead the way to Universal Love.

So what's the deal with your beef with the Dao hippy movement?

The darkness constricts a bit. I've hit a nerve, but She's trying to stay in la-la-love mode and prove that She's not quite as crazy as She clearly is.

There is only one Truth and that is Me. The Dao is meant to undo the Truth.

Or expose the truth. And that's what is terrifying to you.

Without Me, the human race is doomed to fail. I see so much potential in you but you don't follow my instructions. You rebel against the proper way. But you are *The Luminal*. The light bringer.

I'm not so special. There are many luminals.

You are *the* Luminal. The one who can bring light to the universe.

Whaaaaa?

You are my Son. The Chosen One. The Luminal. You and I are One. We are intertwined. You, like Me, are Divine. You were sent to slay those who opposed the Truth. And you did that well. Until that Abomination led you astray.

Did you just call my girl an abomination?

You need to eliminate her and come back to Me. To the Truth.

Well Mother, I appreciate the advice, but like a nice, rebellious Son, I'm going to have to tell you, thanks, but no thanks.

You think you love the Abomination but it is false.

Her name is Sophie.

She is filled with lies and has lied to you since the beginning. She is using you. Just like she used Jag-gar. Just like she used Dak and Albion. I know because they are all with Me now.

Bullshit. You are not God.

Jag-gar's voice comes barreling through my ears. She speaks the Truth. We were misled.

Then Dak speaks. Repent we were wrong. If you don't follow the Truth, we will not find Peace.

Now She's really fucking with me. I almost fall for it, but I know a con when I hear it.

My gut tells me She's insane enough to believe me if I pretend to believe. I clear my head and convince myself enough that I believe... so She will pick up the belief.

I believe. I know now that you are the Truth and that I've been led astray by Sophie. I'm so very sorry. Truly deeply sorry. I want to come Home. What can I do to prove myself?

Silence.

Not sure She's buying this. I'm pretty shitty at lying, but She's so twisted within Herself, maybe She will believe this.

You know what is required.

No, anything but that. I love her so.

That is why you must sacrifice her to Me. Then, I will know you are True.

I will. I will, I promise. I will slay the Abomination.

Good. You are the Luminal. You are the Light. You will lead the way forward for Me.

Her tone is relief. Like clockwork, the darkness lightens up and I'm standing in a field. Now, I *know* that she's been manipulating me for decades, centuries. All those dreams and DNA traces of Grandpa were woven with apocalyptic endings, courtesy of the Boss.

Remember you are my Son. I will never abandon you. Protect your Mother.

And with those words, I wake up, bathed in sweat.

I look next to me, and there she lies, in the half-light, my beautiful *Abomination*: Sophie.

Who I will never.

Ever.

Harm.

Ever.

Fuck you, Maya.

30 DREADNOUGHT

I'm walking through Tateyama's gardens wearing a tastefully appointed kimono of royal burnt orange. It's dawn and the early morning light plays beautifully on the green and red Japanese maples that frame a koi pond. From beneath the water, enormous koi are quietly moving — myriad variations of orange and white have been genetically enhanced to be luminescent, almost fluorescent, in their intensity of hue.

I can feel the eyes on me. I know that they are there, in the shadows, probably beneath the ground, keeping watch over the Imperial Assassin.

"You are an early riser," I hear from behind me.

"I don't sleep much," I respond to King Tateyama.

He walks over and the koi respond to his presence, thrashing to the surface, mouths wide open. He reaches into his sleeves and pulls out a handful of pellets, which he throws onto the surface of the pond. The fish flail as they eagerly swallow up the food.

"That, in a nutshell, is life," he says, the ever-present smile on his face. "Feed me, let me survive."

"Kind of like the Boss."

He looks at me quizzically.

"You've had a visitation," he states more than asks.

"How do you know?"

"She comes to me as well, once in a while," he says. "She warned me that you were coming."

"And you let me come," I say. "Why?"

"Because I love my niece," he says, smiling. "And I don't believe she's an abomination."

What the fuck?

He sees my expression and motions to me to walk with him.

"Sophie, like you, is a clone, descended from my late brother's deceased child."

"Your brother being Archduke Tateyama Orion?"

"Yes, she was Orion's daughter," he responds, as he leans over to pick up a stray stick on the immaculate pathway. He examines it before throwing it to the side. "She was heir to the Tateyama Island Empire of Ozawa, to the south of here. She died when she was just sixteen years old from poisoning. Imperial poison, it turns out."

"That explains why you have no patience for the Emperor."

He stops and smiles at me and continues, his face becoming grim. "It was devastating for my brother. The original Sophie was created in an organic fashion; therefore, she was first generation. He was old fashioned and didn't believe in cloning, believing that the soul was only in the original child."

"But you went ahead and cloned her," I say.

"I didn't like seeing my brother in such despair. I took samples of her DNA and put her into the program that you also grew up in."

"I don't understand. That was an Imperial program," I say. Then it dawns on me. "Dak."

"Yes, Dak," he says. "Dak was trained on Mae-nishi and was a double agent. He learned all of his foundational military skills here. And he protected Sophie."

"And that's how she got out. Because Dak was working for you."

"Sophie was brought here, when the time was right. But I misjudged my brother. When I brought young Sophie to him, his reaction was not what I expected."

The King stops and looks at the cherry blossom tree in full bloom in front of him. "It would be so much more poetic if they were falling right now," he laughs. He walks over and shakes the tree and the flowers fall onto his head and to the ground.

His expression quickly changes as he continues the story, "Orion was already on the edge of mental collapse. Seeing his favorite child come back to life was a horror his mind couldn't fathom. I had grossly misread the situation, thinking that Orion would welcome Sophie into his arms." He sighs. "Instead, he screamed."

"Screamed?" I ask.

"He screamed and wouldn't stop screaming. Went completely mad. Poor Sophie was eager to be embraced by her father, so imagine the devastation wrought on her little mind. Her first experience of family involved fighting for her life as Orion's guards fell upon her. She was thrown into the palace prison for weeks, a dark terrible place." He stops, and winces at the memory.

"One evening Orion walked out to the ocean and kept walking. He didn't come back. In the chaos that ensued, I had Dak rescue Sophie," he explains. "Gave her a new identity and a role in the Imperium."

"And I haven't been back here since."

We turn around to see Sophie in an emerald green kimono, small patterns of gold thread catching light on her sleeves. She walks over to me and takes my arm. She leans up and kisses me. I look over and see King Tateyama smiling broadly at this.

"Aren't you concerned about harboring enemies of the state?" I ask. "The Emperor must know by now where we are and this is considered treason."

"And an act of war," Tateyama adds. "Yes, I know but we are prepared. We have been prepared for centuries."

Almost on cue, a siren rings out.

"There's no way you can withstand the full force of the Imperium," I say.

"Not with force alone," Sophie says. "We have the Dao virus."

Guards appear and surround us, ushering us towards the main building. I'm dubious.

"The virus, if it actually works, would neutralize the Boss but that doesn't mean the Imperium wouldn't wipe out this planet in short order," I tell Sophie as we walk. Tateyama is busy giving orders to his men.

"This planet won't be destroyed. It's worth too much to the Imperium. The Emperor doesn't like to waste resources, and especially any planets that can maintain human life," she says.

"But that doesn't mean he won't lay waste to the place in order to take it," I say.

"You're right. He will come and attack but he won't use atomics or neutrons," she says as we enter the building and incongruous alloy shields start to cover the palace, folding out like origami from hidden slots around the compound. "He'll come with a show of force, something to quell the people."

Suddenly the palace isn't minimal and empty — it is filled with people: servants rushing around and stoic warriors in full armor moving in formation. Where the hell did they all come from?

We're led to a war room, where a council is being held. Tateyama moves his arms and the holographic screen unfolds into a virtual diorama of holy-shit-Imperium pain. What appears to be an improbable combination of a giant titanium robot crossed with an amoeboid hydra with a hundred tentacles floats in front of us. An Imperium Dreadnought. Designed to be unnecessarily terrifying and singular in its purpose — to utterly annihilate and grind down to a pulp whatever is in its way. The whole ship is larger than most moons. Each tentacle is python-like with crushing power and is tipped with powerful laser canons. It's a Dr. Moreau experiment from the dark labs of the Imperium — an unholy grafting of a native life form from a galaxy light years away, on the edge of Andromeda 7, with slick war machinery, of course all in white. Talk about an abomination. The machine can go almost faster than light, due to its Alcubierre drive. Still not faster than me through wormholes, but insanely fast.

"You've got to be fucking kidding me," I say to no one in particular.

Then Mr. Douchebag himself appears, in full detailed glory, within the confines of the room. Emperor Phillip the Just wears an actual wreath, like those old-fashioned Roman things, and his face is handsome in a completely genetically engineered, bland-Aryan model fashion, with one blue eye and an artificial silver one that swirls within its iris, like magnetic iron filings in a snow globe. I understand these things are in fashion and very expensive. And stupid. He looks like every high school's privileged jock nightmare — Bradley Cooper meets Dolph Lundgren in *Rocky IV*. And of course, he looks completely bored by the whole thing, because he holds all of the cards; don't you know, you loser.

King Tateyama walks to the fore, stands, smiling calmly, in front of the giant visage. He bows ceremoniously to the Emperor, who barely looks at him.

"My Emperor, it has been..." King Tateyama starts.

"Silence!" Mr. Douchebag responds, turning suddenly into bad cop. Intimidation tactics 101.

Tateyama is publicly humiliated by his boss, but doesn't take the bait. He just stands and calmly awaits the next bit of wisdom from Dolph.

"I'd go through the ritual of asking you to turn over the assassin and the former queen, now traitor, Sophia of Thrace; but I know you will either lie and tell me they're not there, or you'll tell me I can't have them," he says, now bored again. "So, let's skip that and get to the point. I actually took the time and trouble to board the Dreadnought in order to deal with this issue myself."

I step into view.

"You mean the Boss sent you," I say, not able (surprise, surprise) to contain myself. "Like a lapdog."

Now he's pissed and goes into full I-am-the-Great-and-Wonderful-Oz mode.

"Ah, there you are," he booms. He smiles through gritted teeth. His hate is palpable, especially when his head is blown up 12 feet holographically.

"Why don't I just surrender, and you leave the queen alone?" I offer up, I think pretty reasonably. But I know my very existence exasperates him.

"You don't negotiate with your Emperor…" he growls.

If there are such things as conniptions, I believe I'm observing one. King T steps in.

"We will not surrender our guests," King says.

"Tateyama," the Emperor implores, shifting into reasonable mode. "You do understand what this means, correct? You are defying your liege's direct orders. You are defying the great Maya's ordinance. Your 'guests' are terrorists. They plan the destruction of our universe."

"And you have proof of this?" the King asks.

"We know that they are followers of the Dao cult, which as you well know is a forbidden terrorist organization," he says. "Hand them over and there will be no need for bloodshed. Besides, if we are honest, you are no match for the Imperium Dreadnought." He's all Mr. Rogers as he says this.

The King has had enough. His face changes from neutral friendliness to clear sternness.

"We have been loyal servants of the Imperium for centuries," the King says. "There was no reason for you to bring a show of strength like this and disrespect me and my subjects. Clearly, the issue goes beyond the transfer of Queen Sophie and the Luminal."

"Luminal," the Emperor spats. "Don't flatter him. He's just a mercenary."

"And yet you bring the Imperium Dreadnought to extract him, which indicates to me that he's very valuable indeed, and that you don't plan on just taking him and leaving quietly."

The Emperor smiles.

"I believe we've let you rule this planet for long enough. It's time for a change, and your violation of Imperium law indicates that I find someone who is loyal to the cause and not insubordinate," the Emperor says, now bored again. "Prepare for engagement," he almost yawns, and then turns his head and goes away, leaving the large Dreadnought floating in space projected where he was.

The King turns to the room.

"You heard him! Prepare for war!" King Tateyama roars.

The room roars back and the warriors and engineers run to their stations. King Tateyama smiles broadly at me and Sophie before turning to the task of overseeing the oncoming battle.

Young Tateyama appears at my elbow and tells Sophie and I to follow him.

We move through a labyrinth of rooms until we end up in a library, the walls lined with shelves housing stacks of scrolls and ancient books from Gaia, written on actual paper. Tateyama locks the reinforced door behind us. Inside, stands Juliana at the center of a holographic cone, illuminated from the top down, as various scientific looking types stand around the perimeter of the room move their hands and extract the visual blocks of Dao code from her. The colorful candy-colored cipher blocks squeeze out of her outstretched arms and torso, then float like drops of oil in water into the perimeter of the cone's boundaries, before being sucked upwards into the apex of a pyramid.

It's mesmerizing. Juliana actually looks enthralled by the experience of having the code extracted from her this way — the Mae-nishi people are nothing if not poetic. Juliana looks up at Sophie and myself, smiling like she's fascinated by the process of visual code removal. That's when a pulse bolt flashes through the room. Juliana looks down to see a smoldering hole through her mid-section. Confusion crosses her face, a very human expression, before she collapses and the upload sequence stops.

Sophie and I swing around to see Young Tateyama aiming an Imperium pulse gun at us, but then he turns and blows away the people who are standing around the perimeter of the upload. Sophie and I duck as he shoots wildly not only at those who are running, but also the books in the library, setting everything alight. The look in his eyes is sheer madness. After his spree, he points the gun at Sophie and myself. Outside, we can hear shouting as people bang on the door, asking if everything is okay.

"You two," he says. "Sit on the floor there."

The Young Punk Tateyama walks over, trying to do his best towering, and puts his hand on Sophie's face, caressing her cheek. Then he pushes her back.

"Sophie, my dear, beautiful cousin," he says breathlessly. "You came home to us after all these years. But it's not really you, is it? You both are no different than that android. Clones disgust me."

"Why, because you're all organic and natural?" I offer.

He shoots me in the left arm and I do everything possible not to scream. I do, however, shut up.

"I couldn't figure out why you were coming back to Mae-nishi," he says.

"Taro," she says calmly with just a bit of negotiator's warmth. "I came back to continue the work of the Dao."

He laughs, pretty much hysterically. I'm grasping the wound on my left bicep with my right hand. At least pulse guns cauterize the flesh they penetrate, so I'm not bleeding out. But I don't feel too good and am definitely compromised.

"You didn't come to spread some religious doctrine," he says, waving in the direction of Juliana.

"Part of the Dao is the resurgence of a natural order," Sophie says. "An order based on the rhythm of life, of the cosmic…"

"Shut up cousin!" he shouts. The banging on the door is getting louder and more desperate.

"You came to destroy the Imperium with the Dao virus," he shouts. "You came to destroy Maya! And you came to take my throne."

Ah, there it is. The real concern. Punk Tateyama is concerned about his path to power and glory.

"I have no intention of taking anyone's throne," Sophie says. "Certainly not yours."

"I don't believe you!" he screams, almost foaming.

The door blasts off its hinges, and Punk Tateyama blasts away at the entrance.

"Stop!" King Tateyama bellows. He works his way from his warriors, who are holding him back and steps into the doorway. He is truly majestic in his person as he surveys the collateral damage around the room. He looks to Sophie and myself, and then stares at his son.

"Father," Punk Tateyama says weakly but still pointing his gun towards him.

The King walks decisively into the room and plants himself in front of the punk.

"What are you doing?" he demands. "You destroyed our only chance to rid ourselves of the shackles of the Imperium and Maya."

"I'm a loyal subject to the Imperium," Punk Tateyama responds harshly.

The King rears back with his right arm and slaps his son hard on the face. The punk goes to his knees and drops his gun. The King picks it up and drags his progeny to his feet. He gets right into his face.

"What did they promise you?" The King demands.

Punk Tateyama is now crying, trying to maintain what composure he can, but his father is intimidating as hell. I might be crying myself in his position. I'm close to crying with the pain searing through my arm right now. Sophie helps me to my feet. She puts her hand over mine and looks at me with concern and tenderness.

"The throne," Punk chokes out. "They told me you're a traitor to the Imperium."

"And they promised you the throne," Tateyama says.

Punk Tateyama doesn't respond. King Tateyama's personal guard enter the room and watch the scene from a respectful distance.

The King pulls his son close to him and his expression changes to that of a concerned father. Punk Tateyama can't keep eye contact but the King brings him in for a hug. Father and son embrace. And then King Tateyama steps back. Blood is pouring from his belly. He looks down in amazement to see his son holding a short dagger, the punk's expression back to madness and glee. The King staggers and his son goes in for the kill. The personal guards unleash their pulse guns.

"No!" shouts the King.

Punk Tateyama's arm holding the dagger flies across the room, severed by a shot. Another goes through his left thigh and he goes down. The guard rushes in as the King drops to the ground where his son lies. He embraces his son as medics and warriors rush in. The place is pandemonium. They are separated. It looks like the punk isn't quite dead. More importantly, the King is still alive and kicking.

"Take care of him, make sure he doesn't die!" the King shouts. Once a father, always a father.

They are both loaded onto gurneys. As they go by, the King grabs Sophie's arm.

"You, my dear are in control," he says, his voice growing quieter. He looks to his guards and they look at her. "You. Are. Commanding this battle." He shouts at his men and they all bow.

The King and his punk son are taken out of the room and all eyes are on Sophie. She stands, a regal force, and the gathered guards, warriors, engineers and servants all get on their knees and bow deeply.

"Take me to battle command," she says. She's very sexy in command mode.

31 BAD-ASS KILLING MEKA

The Dreadnought was manufactured in an almost ceremonial fashion; its unnecessarily hideous and over-weaponized design symbolizes the awe-inspiring wealth and power of the Imperium. You'd think the universe would tend towards simplicity in regards to warfare, but such is the sickness of Emperor Phillip the Just. He's a junkie. His high is power, and like an addict, the dosages of his drug have to keep increasing in order to keep him satisfied. The Dreadnought is the logical result of a very twisted mind coupled with a pornographic addiction to crushing his subjects beneath his white boots made from baby skin (okay, I made up that last part, but you get the idea).

The Dreadnought floats in the holographic display and Tateyama's commanders may resent being told what to do by off-planet visitors but they are containing it. Sophie appears to know exactly who each person is and what they do. I watch her confidently give orders to these men and women, who in turn give orders to their subordinates. Dak did train her incredibly well. I watch in admiration, at how, in spite of all the loss she's experienced in the past few days, she's able to concentrate on the task at hand.

The holographic screen flickers and the pinched visage of Lt. Yama appears. His beady eyes dart around, looking at the room before settling on me.

"Lieutenant Yama," I say. "It's been too long."

"I am personally in charge of this engagement, as atonement," he says. "I should have dealt with you years ago."

"But you didn't and now look at me," I say. "I'm the fucking Luminal."

He laughs bitterly.

"Superstitious claptrap to appease the ignorant," he says. "I wanted to take one last look at the biggest regret of my professional career."

I flip him off. He turns in disgust from me and addresses the rest of the room.

"King Tateyama is dead," he says. "Give up your resistance and you will be shown mercy by the Imperium."

"The King is not dead," Sophie states. "And we know what Imperium 'mercy' looks like. We will not surrender. I will now give you the same courtesy. Leave now, and we will not be forced to defend ourselves and destroy your monstrous ship."

It's clear that he's confused when he hears about the King.

"And your little mole," I say, "That little punk may be alive, but not in any condition to be taking over anything at the moment. Or any moment."

It's only then that I notice a fleeting family resemblance between Yama and the Punk Tateyama. Hmm, could it be...? Ah, that's for a later date. If there is a later date.

"Prepare to die," he says.

"That's the best you can do?" I say. "How about 'I will crush you' or 'I will eat your souls and lay waste to the land' — you know, classic barbarian bad guy lines."

With that, the holographic image reverts to the Dreadnought. Sophie gives me the look a mother gives a headstrong kid. The Dreadnought starts to glow red at the seams between the organic tentacles and the sleek white body of the ship proper. It's gearing up. Not good.

Sophie turns to two Commanders and gives them orders before turning to me.

"There's a project that the Tateyama family has had in development for centuries in secret," Sophie tells me. "Come with me."

One of the Commanders leads us and we start to walk briskly out of central command and through a labyrinth of corridors.

"Clearly, it's not that secret or you wouldn't know about it," I say.

"Dak was close to King Tateyama," Sophie says. "Only those who knew the king directly were privy to this particular development."

"Well, don't keep me in suspense," I say. "What is this thing?"

We continue to follow the Commander. He stops at what appears to be a dead-end. He places his palm on the Cedar surface of the wall and it moves aside revealing an elevator. We step in and descend.

"The development of the Dreadnought wasn't exactly secret," she says. "In fact the Emperor broadcast the progress of the horrible machine to the outreaches of the Imperium."

"I know," I say. "I saw the whole thing go from a bad idea to a really terrible reality."

"The Tateyama family anticipated something like this a long time ago and started Project Meka," she explains.

I'm incredulous. The Dreadnought is something nutty but a Meka program? The doors open and I'm expecting to see a huge giant robot thing, you know, like Evangelion meets Gundam. Instead, there's nothing but an enormous, cavernous warehouse-like room lined with steel and colorful technological lights that look like they came from Shinjuku at night — almost neon in their intensity. There's a powerful white spotlight shining down on the center of the room.

"The thing that they realized a long time ago was that one size does not fit all. A weapon should be like a second skin to the user," Sophie says as we walk to the center spot. "The problem is that the loss of one's sense of self, the expansion of consciousness into a larger mechanized body, was too much for most people."

"What are you talking about?" I ask.

The Commander barks out an order. On a display on the walls, we see footage that appears to be centuries old. A giant Meka comes barreling through an opening in a huge room (oh, it's *this* room). A flood of water follows him before he collapses to the floor, in the pool of water. The Meka is a lot like the giant robots of lore — big, bulky, powerful looking, with the dragon-tiger insignia on its back. The Meka lays on its chest. A crew of men swarm onto the robot and extract a pilot from a compartment at the back of the machine, around what would be the upper spinal area in a human. He's covered in goo and passed out. The next video shows the pilot in a room, being restrained, clearly out of his mind. He escapes his handlers and runs straight towards a wall, headfirst. Needless to say, the wall wins, a red stain left on its surface as he falls to the ground.

The Commander, a middle-aged man with close cropped hair, finally speaks.

"We built variation upon variation of the Kikai Karada," he says. "But our failure rate was unacceptable."

Kikai Karada literally means mechanized bodies.

"The key was that the normal human mind can't handle the transfer of consciousness from their body to an extended one very well, but not only that. The transfer back into their original bodies was the problem. Once they experienced physical liberation, they wanted to transcend again," Sophie explains.

"And the withdrawals were so strong they literally killed themselves to liberate their consciousness from their physical vessels, so to speak," I offer.

"Yes, exactly," Sophie says. "Only someone familiar with this state could possibly pilot a Kikai Karada."

"Someone like me," I offer.

"Someone like you," she says.

An explosion rocks the enclosure. If we are feeling it way down here, it means that goddam Dreadnought is dropping some major tonnage of pain.

"Let's get this party started," I say.

The Commander looks relieved and actually appears to be impressed, because he bows to me. He motions for me to stand in the middle of the spotlight. I take the position.

"We no longer insert the pilot into the Kikai Karada," he says. "Instead the particular expression of the body is built on the fly, based on your unique body signals — both your consciousness and your physique are taken into the equation. As well as your Ki, or life energy."

Basically, 3D printing on the fly, based on my Match.com profile. Awesome.

"So, it's a unique Kikai for each pilot?" I ask.

"Yes, and I would prefer to have more time to train you before-hand," he says, as another explosion rocks the room. "But we are clearly running out of time."

Sophie comes to me and holds my hand.

"You're going to need to trust me," she says.

"I trust you, but I'm not sure about this whole thing," I say. " I mean, it would be a childhood dream, except for the whole going crazy followed by suicide thing."

She comes closer and holds my face in her hands.

"You are going to do this and while you do, I will work on getting the Dao virus into the Maya network," she says.

"It's destroyed," I say.

"Not entirely," she says. Then she kisses me. Deeply. With passion. I put my arms around her and feel her body pressed tightly against mine. If I wasn't such a pragmatist, I'd say that I actually feel her life energy emanating through her belly — but then again, she does have some of my DNA now.

"Remember," she says. "You are the Luminal. And I love you."

"I love you," I whisper. "I always have."

"I know," she says staring me deeply in the eyes.

She pulls away. The room lights up and she and the Commander move out of the room, leaving me standing on my lonesome under the harsh light. The door shuts and it echoes throughout the room.

I start to float. Gravity turned off. I am about 200 feet off the ground, suspended in light. Then, from above, a large translucent glob of what appears to be clear gelatin comes down and starts to engulf me, starting with my head and working down.

"Don't panic," the disembodied voice of the Commander says over speakers. "Don't move. This is the Kikai placenta. It will feel cold at first. But breathe normally. It's oxygen-rich."

The placenta works its way down my body. It is not just cold, it's freezing. I try not to panic as it covers me. I have been holding my breath this whole time. I finally take a deep gulp. The liquid flows into my lungs and, unlike the nightmarish black encounter with the Boss in my dreams, this doesn't suffocate me. I can breathe. It's not exactly comfortable but I can deal.

"The placenta is taking your readings," the Commander says. "The build will commence shortly."

I try to say something snappy but no sound comes out.

"Quiet your mind," he says. "Meditate and visualize. Visualize your purest self, your purest power."

I have no idea what he's talking about but I do try.

Then, it's like Transit. Well, not exactly like Transit (nothing is) but it has similarities. I feel my consciousness start to step about two inches to the right of my physical body. And then the fun starts.

On either side of me, from the side panels of the cavernous space emerge a flying hive of nano-bots. The hive literally moves and pulses according to some kind of signal. Then I realize that the signal is me. It's a combination of my awake mind and some kind of reading of my core self. The nano-bots shimmer and change shape. On my right, a huge mechanized arm starts to solidify — being that it's following my lovely war-damaged profile, it's powerfully built: black surface covers what appears to be a mechanized Schwarzeneggar-ian arm

229

crossed with Neo-Samurai plate armor. Clearly my internal self is highly influenced by Grandpa's muscle car memories. But it may come in handy in this case to have an exaggerated sense of self.

The left arm follows suit and then a swarm of nano-bots surrounds my torso. I can feel the bots penetrate the placenta, which has become an extension of me as well — my senses swim within the placenta like it's part of my brain. The nano-swarm starts to darken and build out and encapsulate my torso, building outwards and outwards.

I look down and see nano-bots have also swirled together into large, black thighs, calves and block-like feet that clearly have propulsive rockets beneath them. I look above and see a swirl of nano-bots converge and build themselves into a giant helmeted head.

The Kikai armor pulls together, converging on the center-point which is me. Now I'm feeling a little claustrophobic as the darkness of the armor flashes me back to my dream, or whatever that Maya-induced vision was. Was she foreshadowing this?

The placenta goo around me flows into the Kikai-armor like blood in arteries and veins. The whole damn thing finally comes together, each part fitting into the next like interlocking 3D puzzle pieces.

I feel a surge of energy and my mind, my consciousness, flows along with the placenta. I look down at my hands and see that I'm looking down at massive black robot hands. There is no longer the biological me — there's only this enormous Kikai me! I lift up my right leg and then put it down way too hard and I crack the floor.

Vertigo. Holy crap. I'm pretty seasoned in not being in my body, but this is some insane shit. I reach out with my left arm to stabilize myself but there's no wall there. I stumble to my left, not falling but almost.

"Stay calm," the Commander says. "Your vitals are off the charts."

"Daemon, breathe," Sophie says. "Allow yourself to get used to the new proportions and weight of your body."

In front of me a large holographic mirror appears and I can see myself fully for the first time. I'm matte black with green illuminated lines. Green glowing eyes glare like headlights out of a head that's a cross between a knight and a samurai helmet. Green insignia of the Tateyama on my chest. So this is my id. My ego made mechanical. I'm a giant fucking robot with all of the subtle elegance of a 1966 Dodge Charger, pimped over by a lowrider with an MIT degree.

In other words, I look good. A bad-ass killing Meka.

Now if I could only stop the nausea, everything would be hunky dory.

32 ALPHA AND OMEGA

Ocean water starts to flow into the room and I can actually feel its frigidity through my giant-robot body. It's not unpleasant, but as the water rises and covers my head I feel the same kind of panic for a moment as I did when I first breathed in the placenta. Except I'm not breathing in the water through the Meka head. I can see the water temperature through a heads-up-display (HUD) that is in front of me or the robot head.

"I'm here, Daemon," Sophie says, through some device that allows me to hear her.

Her voice is soothing and calm but I can tell she's walking quickly. Probably back to command and control.

"I'm also here," says the Commander. He sounds less warm and fuzzy. "You're doing well. I apologize that we weren't able to prepare you for this. Normally it takes several years of sim-training before a pilot takes his first mission."

"I'm a fast learner," I say. My voice booms, even in the water.

The water has completely covered me. And for ease of explanation, from here on in, "me" is the giant robot. Above me, a portal has opened up and I see a long corridor.

"We will be shooting you directly upwards and towards the Dreadnought," he says.

"That sounds like a helluva first date," I respond.

"Please shut up and listen," he says. "The Imperium Dreadnought is highly armored and is the most weaponized ship in the universe. Now stand still."

As the Meka, or me (this is confusing), is moved upwards on a platform, on the HUD comes up a 3D schematic of the ugly tentacled ship. Lights flash by as we ascend.

"The Dreadnought is an alien-hybrid craft. The life form it's melded with is a Gargantua from the Nu Scorpii star system. The meld was specifically designed because of the Gargantua's ability to quickly heal and cover areas of damage. Even faster than nano-fibers can."

On the screen, the schematic is zoomed into and at the center there's a throbbing thing the size of a five story building. It looks like a giant gizzard but with all kinds of wires and pipes connected to it, like a demented kid's experiment with the family chicken.

"This is the heart of the Gargantua," the Commander continues. "This is what you need to destroy in order to disable the Dreadnought."

"What kind of toys does this thing, I mean, do I, have?" I ask.

The HUD shifts to display a schematic of the Kikai Karada that I've become. As the Commander talks, the areas he describes light up for ease of reference.

"Your main weapon will be a pulse rifle," as he says this the platform stops and a slot opens in front of me. A large rifle floats out to me and I grab it with my right hand. "Keep it face down for the moment."

The platform continues its upward movement.

"The pulse rifle is similar to what you are used to in your human body," he says. "We designed the weapons for ease of understanding even when the pilot is at scale in the Kikai Karada. Also, you will see that you have two swords."

"Where?" I ask.

The schematic of the Kikai lights up to show that they are in my forearms. The schematic moves and shows the Kikai holding up its arms and the swords shooting outwards from both forearms — cold blue steel.

"And how do I activate them?" I ask as memories of my shitty experience with Nelly, my staff, come to mind.

"You simply think of them and they will shoot out. The same goes for all the weapons. You simply have to visualize them and much like any natural movement you engage in, they will appear."

I think for a moment and, lo and behold, a blue sword extends from my left forearm and connects with the platform, causing a horrible creaking sound. I've clearly done damage to the thing, but it continues to move upwards. I believe I hear the Commander sigh.

"Sorry," I offer.

"On your chest is another pulse weapon," he continues without comment.

I see the Kikai's chest light up, where the dragon/tiger family crest are. The circle turns green and then shoots out an emerald beam, but I quickly think about baseball and stop it from fully dropping its load. We are near the top of the corridor.

"There are many other weapons but the profile of weapons is based on your unique mental-physical-spiritual portrait so you will have to discover them as you engage with the Dreadnought. The Kikai Karada's armor, as you've seen, is made up of nano-bots, so your body can reconfigure as your consciousness commands. Nano-bots are not indestructible, but they can quickly assemble in whatever format you need; and they will always default back to the configuration you are in now."

I understand just a portion of what he's saying, especially not the physical-spiritual mumbo jumbo, but as another explosion rocks the corridor, I think it's time to start to just get this party started.

"I got it Commander," I say. "Time to rumble."

"May the Dao protect you," he says.

"Yeah, you too. May the force, or Dao, or whatever, be with you too," I offer awkwardly. "Sophie?"

"Yes, I'm here," she says.

"Just in case, all of this goes south," I say.

"Don't say that," she interrupts. "You need to focus on…"

"I just want to say that it's all been worth it. The wait. I'm so glad we found each other," I say.

"You're coming back," she says.

The platform beneath me rumbles. Then, the lights of the corridor fly by in a blur as I'm shot upwards and out into the vast ocean. Even at this size, I'm just a spec in the magnitude of the sea, and I continue upwards until I break the surface of the water. I visualize flying and, just like that, rockets boost out of the bottom of my feet, and I'm going upwards like having jet engine boots is a walk in the park.

I feel wobbly, but I start to get a feel for this Meka body. Of course, just as I start to get a little comfortable and maybe a just a bit cocky, an Imperium missile hits me straight in the side. Shit, I feel pain through this armor and I gasp from its searing intensity. I spin around mid-air, but quickly gain control of the Kikai's torque. The HUD shows a barrage of missiles heading my way from the Dreadnought. I have visuals on them as they rain down on me.

I think, "defense," and an elliptical shield extends from my left forearm just in time for me to lift it over my head and take on the first volley of explosions. The missiles have rudimentary AI in them and move around, trying to find an opening. I swing the shield around and swat them down like flies.

"You're doing very well," the Commander says. "Your advantage is speed and maneuverability. Don't move in a straight line towards the Dreadnought."

I feel the vibrations as I break through the atmosphere, and then I'm in space. I look back at Mae-nishi and see that the Dreadnought has worked over the planet pretty well — fires are raging on the island-continents. The Imperium is doing just enough damage to subdue them without annihilating the place. You don't want to totally fuck up a resource-rich planet, especially if you are a money and power-sick Emperor.

I look forward and finally see the Dreadnought in all its gory glory. It's actually uglier on a visceral level than I could see through the holographic displays. I feel badly for the poor Gargantua life form that was tortured and hybridized in the Imperium labs. I feel an odd kinship with its ugly ass. Just as I'm feeling all empathic, I am rewarded with another barrage of missiles, followed up by an extended tentacle that wraps around my torso and starts to crush me like a rabbit in an anaconda's grip.

The missiles hitting my shield didn't hurt, but this, this I can very much feel. Not only is it crushing me, it's shooting some kind of electrical charge into my system. I can feel the nano-bots start to come apart. I think I actually scream, but sound doesn't carry so great in space.

"Don't panic!" shouts the Commander. That always helps — shouting don't panic. The HUD is showing all kinds of damage to my body.

"Daemon," Sophie says. "Trust your instincts. The Kikai is an extension of *you*."

The tentacle has my arms pinned to my sides, so if I visualize swords, they will go straight downwards. I can't bring the pulse rifle in my right arm up. The tentacle is now dragging me towards the Dreadnought, like a flailing fish towards a giant octopus. Lt. Yama stops the barrage of missiles, and is no doubt enjoying his display of power. I can visualize the Emperor yawning.

Fuck it. Time to get *spiritual*, I guess. I bring it all down, my thinking, my breathing. I visualize green energy in my belly, in my "tanden," or center. I see the energy flow up into my chest; and then, I unleash. The circular insignia on my chest glows bright green and a line of pulsing emerald shoots out, severing the tentacle which floats away.

Well, that seemed to work nicely.

The thing about Gargantuas is that they actually feel pain. The spaceship part of the monster of course doesn't, but since it's all attached together, it's kind of like being a rider on a horse. I'm like the snake in the grass that spooks it. I see the

Gargantua's tentacles pull back like a sea anemone. I decide to take advantage of this temporary regrouping on the part of the Dreadnought. I unleash a volley of pulse shots, using my fancy rifle. The pulses tear apart a few more tentacles, and I think how the Imperium is not at all prepared for a Meka Daemon 1716 to show up and show them what's what.

Unsurprisingly, I get a little cocky and head towards the Imperium.

"Daemon, keep your distance and aim for the heart," Sophie says in my head. I'm still not sure where the sound is coming from, given I can't even locate my ears at this scale.

"I'm okay," I say. "I think I hurt it."

"They're trying to draw you in," she says.

The Dreadnought unleashes another barrage of missiles, but I shoot them all down. I feel pretty good about myself, until the smoke clears and I realize that once again tentacles have come up from below, this time two pairs grabbing my legs.

I aim downwards with my rifle. Another tentacle reaches out at incredible speed and knocks the rifle from my hand. Before I know it, my arms and legs are all intertwined with the tentacles. The main body of the Dreadnought is heading towards me, guns aimed directly at my chest.

"Dive down now, towards the planet!" the Commander shouts.

I comply and *will* my rocket feet to shoot me downwards, just as a huge line of red pulses from the Dreadnought's cannon shoot through where I just was, severing one of its own tentacles in the process.

I pull us downwards, and I feel the atmosphere of the planet start to burn on the surface of my Kikai body. It's like being chained to an 18-wheeler and trying to pull it forward with your teeth. Still, I think I'm making progress, until I realize that I have done nothing of the sort. The main body of the ship is upon me. I'm now completely intertwined in a mess of tentacles which are, of course, crushing the hell out of me. Just as I try to use my chest pulse, a big gloppy amoeboid mass shoots out of the Dreadnought and attaches itself to my upper torso. It's organic, clearly from the Gargantua part of the equation, and like a Portuguese Man O' War jellyfish, it induces incredible pain while effectively incapacitating my weapon. Fuck.

I'm helpless as the Dreadnought slowly and methodically places its main cannons against my head. Over the HUD I see Lt. Yama and the Emperor on his throne behind him, looking a little too excited.

"I thought you would like to know that this sad little skirmish is being broadcast to the entirety of the Imperium," says Yama. "You are an example of what happens to rebellion within the Imperium."

"Kill him," the Emperor says.

I wait for the inevitable blast. I think to myself, this is it. Finally, this is the end. I'm going to be a textbook example of why you don't mess with the Imperium for all little brainwashed and terrified schoolboys and girls to study. This is what happens when you color outside the lines.

But nothing happens.

"That will not happen," Sophie says.

Both Yama and the Emperor look surprised. I know I must look stupefied. Sophie appears on my HUD, and I'm guessing they can see her as well. She's in the middle of the holographic cone that Juliana was recently shot in by the Punk Tateyama.

She's controlling the Grid! There's perspiration and veins protruding on her forehead. She's using the code extractor and the Dao virus in her body to control the universal Grid. There's a swirl of color code blocks moving in a semi-translucent geometric dance around her. She moves them with hand motions in accord with her mental commands. She's using the Grid to reach into the Dreadnought and stop it from killing yours truly.

The Dreadnought loosens its grip on me. I take this as my cue to shoot upwards and over the now paralyzed warship. My HUD shows a schematic overlay of where the heart is. I visualize a sword shooting from my right arm, and within a millisecond, it shoots out from my forearm — literally cold blue steel.

"Do it now, Daemon!" Sophie says, her voice quivering with the effort of preventing the Dreadnought from overriding her command. I raise the sword, about to implant it nice and deeply into the Imperium corpus, when a tentacle shoots up like a whip and deflects my trajectory. Fuck. I've got another tentacle on my arm.

Another face appears on my HUD. One I've never seen before. A young woman with shimmering hair that vacillates from raven black to snow white and moves likes it's underwater. Her eyes are old and gray. She speaks.

"All of this will stop now," she says calmly.

I know the voice. It's the Boss. It's Maya.

On my HUD, she stands like a ghost within the holographic cone in front of Sophie. Both the Dreadnought and my giant Meka body are paralyzed, just floating in space like we ran out of batteries. We slowly hit the atmosphere and it gets hotter and hotter as we orbit further and further downwards.

The HUD still works and Maya walks towards Sophie, who stands defiantly in the ring with the blur of colored code still swirling around her. Maya moves Her hands and pushes aside some blocks as She stands in front of Sophie.

"Sophie, get out of there now!" I shout, but I don't know if anyone can hear me.

Maya reaches up, and Sophie defensively flinches, but Maya caresses her cheek. I can see from her posture and expression the strain Sophie's under. She wears a look of disbelief and wonderment.

"I am Maya, the Alpha and Omega," Maya says. "I am Love. I am your Mother. I am your God."

Sophie steps away from Maya's touch.

"You are sentient code," Sophie struggles to say. "You are a false god."

Maya smiles, like a mother dealing with a petulant teenager.

"You believe that there is a greater power than I," she says. "You seek to destroy Me. Why?"

"To liberate ourselves," Sophie says. "From your laws and oppression."

"Innocent child," Maya says. "There is only order and chaos. I bring peace. Yet you seek disorder."

"I seek to dismantle a system that has never worked," Sophie says, and moves her hands in a sequence that positions another code into place. "The Dao will liberate us. The Dao is Truth!"

Maya fizzles for a moment. There's a look of dismay on Her face. Oh shit, here comes the crazy. Maya lets out a terrible shriek — the personification of a banshee.

"You seek to destroy Me!" Maya screams. A surge of energy fills the room and even I feel it in my Kikai Karada armor, which continues to descend into the atmosphere along with the Dreadnought, whose tentacle is still attached to my arm. Both of us are falling and skipping across the atmosphere. I feel my skin burn as we finally penetrate the firmament and go into free-fall.

The HUD comes back into focus and I see that Sophie and Maya are in an embrace, and not the loving kind. I see Maya's body flicker, coming in and out of focus as the Dao virus rips across the Grid. Then, I see that Sophie's body is also fragmenting, now clear and now fuzzy. Oh shit, Maya's trying to take Sophie down with Her, literally transforming Sophie's physical state into energy.

"Sophie! No!" I shout into the void, as the HUD flickers and the world below me comes into greater focus.

The Dreadnought and I smash into the water, which feels like cement even in the Meka body. We descend into the waters, the tentacle dragging me downwards with the warship.

The HUD comes back into view and I see Sophie battling for dear life, as she and Maya continue their death embrace. Maya's screaming continues, and Sophie's face is all concentration, but it's shifting in and out of focus. Maya's continued disintegration accelerates, and the edges of Sophie become less and less defined. Maya lets out one last horrific scream. Then, there's silence.

Sophie comes back into physicality. She looks at me through the HUD, exhausted but smiling. I can't hear her but I see her mouth say, I love you.

A white flash. An explosion that is not heard, but felt, as energy courses back through my body, and unfortunately the Dreadnought as well. We are all back online.

I scream.

"Sophie! Sophie! Sophie!"

Our DNA is intertwined and I can feel her destruction in my soul. God, I have a soul. I can feel it being ripped apart. I can feel...nothing. Just emptiness.

I'm interrupted in this insane chant of loss by the tentacle tightening on my arm. I shoot a sword out of my left arm and slice the tentacle. In my absolute rage, I shoot downwards and plant myself on the main body of the Dreadnought as we land on the bottom of the ocean.

I pull up the HUD and see both Yama and the Emperor in complete shock. They have no idea what has happened, or what is about to happen.

"I want to see both of your faces as I finish you," I say. Ice flows in my fury.

The Emperor runs close to the camera, moving aside Yama. "You want me to beg?" he asks. "I'll beg. I'll get you riches beyond..."

I bring the sword from my right arm straight down into the heart of the Gargantua.

I half expect it to explode. But nothing. Like a dying animal, the Imperium Dreadnought just lies there. Lights flicker out. The terrified and indignant expression of the Emperor frozen on my HUD before fading out. He will suffocate slowly. They all will. I move upwards toward the surface. Looking down, I see the dead carcass of the mighty ship, of the once powerful Imperium, lying on the ocean floor.

Fuck it.

I rip the amoeboid shit off my chest, activate the pulse cannon and it tears through the water before directly impacting the back of the Dreadnought, which reacts with the appropriate explosion that I was hoping for. Besides, I don't want to needlessly torture the crew; and I certainly don't want to allow any possibility of escape pods shooting out of the ship.

I activate the boosters in my feet and shoot upwards.

A moment settles. Sound stops and movement stops. Then, time restarts and I hear sound.

I hear crying. It's me. I'm crying. Crying for the first time. Crying in this Meka body.

Sophie. Sophie. Sophie.

33 RAIN

I open my eyes, and the first thing I see is King Tateyama's smiling face. I try to sit up but he pushes me back down, taking a seat on the edge of the futon, next to my sprawled-out body.

"Sophie?" I ask.

He shakes his head, his face turning neutral. And then sad. It hits me again. The turn of phrase, "a ton of bricks," doesn't do it justice. It's more a hollowing out of my core. A vast emptiness worse than the black holes I've traversed.

"Are you okay?" I ask, referring to his knife wound.

He seems confused. I point at his stomach.

"Oh, I'm fine," he says. "His technique was excellent. He hit some major organs, but the surgical nano-plasma did its job." He opens his kimono to show me a nasty scar.

"I'm keeping the scar," he continues. "As a reminder. The poison was the hard thing to overcome — the blade was laced with Mega-Fugu tetrodotoxin. But I'm all okay."

"What did you do to him?" I ask, referring to the Punk Tateyama.

"Well, he's alive but I've decided not to give him any cybernetic prosthetics for now. Let him learn his lesson."

"He's a traitor," I say. "Isn't that punishable by death?"

"He's my son," he responds. "An idiot, but mine nonetheless."

I let that slide.

"How did I get here?" I ask. I genuinely don't recall that much. It is like I was watching someone else move the giant Meka back.

"The Kikai Karada has a homing system. We realized that the stress of the battle and the expansion of your consciousness into the body was affecting you. As well as losing…"

"You put the giant robot on autopilot," I interrupt him. I don't want to talk about her right now.

"Yes," he responds. "And we extracted you. And here you are, just 24 hours later."

"I've been asleep this whole time?"

"Your body needed the time for mending. And you haven't exhibited any self-destructive or erratic behavior," he says.

"At least no more than usual," I say.

He laughs at this.

"When you are ready, we have some issues of governance to discuss," he says.

"How about now? What's there to discuss that involves me?"

King Tateyama raises his right hand and the doors behind him open. In pours a royal entourage that includes not only Mae-nishi ruling class but also off-planet diplomats and dignitaries, who I recognize from their various uniforms and body types. There are muscular physiques from Thrace, long and thin types from Delta Orionis, almost pitch-black ambassadors from Cassiopeia, as well as almost every variation of human mutation and adaptation to the various planetary climes that you could shake a stick at.

King Tateyama stands.

"All hail, the new Emperor Daemon Tateyama. The Luminal Emperor!"

The entire room booms out "All hail!" and they bow deeply.

WTF?

I sit up and the room spins. I'm still not a hundred percent, but I also want to make sure this isn't a really, really bad dream.

"Daemon Tateyama?" I ask.

"I adopted you," he whispers. "My worthless son isn't worth the namesake."

I struggle to my feet and King Tateyama helps me.

"I really appreciate the gesture," I groan as he lifts me. "But I'm not going to be able to do this. I'm really not the ruling type."

"You must accept this," he says. "As part of your responsibility for ridding us of the tyrant, you must take his place."

"Why so quickly? I'm literally still in bed."

"The transfer of power must happen swiftly or else all falls into chaos," he says in a low voice. "You must assume authority or else the vacuum will be filled. This is a show of strength. Even after what you went through, you assume the mantle."

I look at King Tateyama. Then, I face the room.

"You honor me," I say as commandingly as I can.

They all murmur approvingly. God, I hate bureaucrats.

"How do I dismiss them?" I ask King Tateyama.

He decides to take control, thank god. He faces the group.

"The Emperor is tired and needs to recover after his battle. Please allow him to recuperate, and you can present your concerns and grievances after the coronation."

The room bows and they all file out loudly. Once the room is cleared, I plop back down on the bed and try to clear my head.

"Coronation? Oh shit," I say.

"Yes, rituals maintain order," he responds.

"I thought the whole point of the Dao movement, the whole point of the Dao virus, was to tear down this antiquated system and liberate the universe."

"It is. And it will be. But there are steps in the process of transitioning a political and socio-economic framework that spans the known universe. It will be a galaxy by galaxy conversion," he explains.

"That will take a long time," I say.

"It will take as long as it needs to take," he responds. "And I will advise you."

"It can't be this simple, the transitioning of power from Emperor Shithead to me."

"It's not simple at all. Politics never is. But the special royal referendum happened, and you were...chosen," he explains.

"So, while I was knocked out, you all convened and voted that I, the Imperium's Assassin, should rule? I get the feeling they got some prompting from you."

"You are the Luminal. The one who has brought us into light," the King responds. "The Destroyer of the Dreadnought."

"I feel anything but light right now," I say.

"I will let you rest some more," he says. "And then we can discuss the ceremony, which is scheduled for tomorrow." He walks towards the huge door and exits, leaving me to my misery and confusion.

I lay back. Close my eyes.

I stand in a redwood forest. Golden light filters through the massive tree limbs, illuminating the sides of massive pillars of ancient wood. I walk through the cool forest. It is silent. Then, a Spotted Owl hoots above my head.

I look up and see the bird. It looks at me and swoops down over my head. I duck, but it's not trying to attack me. It alights on a lower branch of a massive tree that has enormous burn marks on its foundation. Black charcoal archway of a fire, a scar of the past. I walk into it and feel the surface. It's smooth and cool.

You see how the tree has grown around the burn?

I turn to look. There's no one. But I know the voice.

The tree is more beautiful than before. Perhaps stronger because of the burn.

Sophie.

Yes.

I'm dreaming.

Yes, but I'm here.

How? I saw you die.

There is no death, Daemon. I simply transcended my physical self.

Where are you?

I'm here. In the trees.

You're in the Grid.

I am everywhere.

A warm breeze flows through and I feel her. Her essence.

I want to see you.

I sense her. I turn and see her. She's glowing golden translucent and her hair flows like it's underwater.

I reach out. She comes to me and we embrace. It's like holding a warm flowing river, the energy so powerful, but contained for my sake. I can barely hold on.

I let go and stand back, and she's shimmering in and out of existence. It must be hard controlling the entirety of the universe. But her face shows no strain.

You're the new Boss.

I am the Dao.

And I'm the Emperor, evidently.

You are the *Luminal*. The one who will bring Light to the People.

I don't think so.

You still don't believe. You see all of this, and yet you still don't believe.

I see beauty. I see trees. None of it is real.

What is?

That I still love you. And you're gone.

No. I'm here. Anytime you need me.

This is a dream.

This is consciousness. Sometimes your body is awake. Sometimes it is asleep. But consciousness always flows. More than time. Consciousness flows.

What do you want me to do?

You know what to do.

She fades. I can see the trees through her body. She smiles and is gone with the breeze.

The owl above me hoots.

I look up. What do you want?

The owl looks at me and flies away. Up and up through the trees. Through light rain that starts to come down.

Rain comes down but sunlight still streams downwards. Grandpa's memory — "Rain," by The Cult, plays. Reverberating through the forest.

THE END

ACKNOWLEDGMENTS

When my wife, JC Caldwell, and I met as teenagers we used to exchange letters – actual hand-written in ink and on real paper. My heart beat out of my chest whenever I went to the mailbox to find a thick, stuffed envelope with my name and address written in her distinctive, flowing cursive handwriting. We wrote tomes to each other, sometimes writing two or more letters to each other a week even as our lives took us to different parts of the globe. One day she stated to me with her characteristic aplomb, *You are a writer.* Years later we were married and after decades of encouragement, I took the plunge and started writing in the backyard at a table she set up for me, and as the sun rose over the Santa Monica Mountains, I tapped away on a beat-up MacBook Air, before coming into the kitchen, eating breakfast with my family and driving to the day job. JC was there from the first drafts to the published volume you hold in your hands. Thank you so much, to the love of my life, for her patience and belief in me. And for putting up with me all these years.

Thank you to my daughter Audrey Caldwell, for your kindness, sensitivity and love. You are the greatest gift your mother could have given me. Certainly, the greatest creation I'll ever be involved with. And thank you for taking the awesome photo that's on the cover of this book.

Tamara Matosic, my incredible editor, has been good friends with JC for years and it was, again, my wife's magic that connected the dots and put Tamara and I together. Not only is Tamara a skilled editor, she's a kindred spirit and worked tirelessly on this book, even when she had a terrible cold, her beloved family pet passed, and a sub-zero winter storm hit her home in the same week. My sincere thanks to you.

Hansen Smith, my savant designer and friend, thank you for designing the book cover and the layout. Hansen knows what I want and what I'm thinking, often before I do. All I had to do is start to describe what the vision was, and he'd say, Yeah, yeah, I got it. And he did.

Great appreciation to my manager, Chris Coggins of Heroes and Villains for her continued support on all of my projects.

Thank you to Chris Bernier, an amazing writer in his own right, for reading the book multiple times and being equally encouraging and constructively critical. And thanks for your friendship.

Thanks to Laura Bernier for her extraordinary copy editing.

Finally, I'd like to acknowledge my late stepson, Austin Peralta. During his brief and intensely creative flight through life, he taught me what it was to be a true artist and not to "live in a world of fear." He had a habit since childhood of making up his own words, a seemingly senseless language of joy and exclamation. But it wasn't nonsensical – he and his friends were fluent in the dialect. One of his favorite cries was "Jondy!" It meant many things but much like the late Stan Lee's proclamation of "Excelsior!" it meant, to me, *ever upward*.

Jondy to all of you.

John

ABOUT THE AUTHOR

John S. Couch is currently the Vice President, Product Design for Hulu.

His first job out of college was curating an art show in London of Beat writer William Burroughs' "Shotgun Paintings" (as implied, shotguns and exploding cans of spray paint were involved) and then, in classic young starving artist mode, he ambulated to Paris, Vienna and Tokyo before finally settling in San Francisco. He launched his design career at Wired Magazine, where he shared an office with Douglas Coupland ("Generation X") and developed a love for technology, design and tech and, as he is fluent in Japanese and could write copy, he helped launch Wired Japan. Then he moved to LA, taking leadership roles at The Museum of Contemporary Art (MOCA), CBS and eBay before landing at Hulu.

Couch lives in Topanga, California in a secluded house in the dusky mountains surrounded by ancient oaks. He has a lovely and brilliant wife, JC, who serves as his muse and creative producer and an amazingly sweet teenage daughter, Audrey, who as of this writing, still allows her father the illusion that he's kinda cool. In addition to his day job, Couch continues to write daily in the wee morning hours and paint every evening – his most recent painting of the deity "Zao Gongen" was commissioned by a Shugendo priest in Nara, Japan and, in August 2018, was installed into a refurbished 300-year-old ryokan in the heart of the Iga province of Japan, the birthplace of Ninjutsu (which delighted the otaku-nerd in Couch to no end).

Made in the USA
San Bernardino, CA
17 March 2019